Seasons of the Heart

Seasons of the Heart

Book Two
of the Enduring Faith Series

SUSAN C. FELDHAKE

ZondervanPublishingHouse
Grand Rapids, Michigan
A Division of HarperCollinsPublishers

Seasons of the Heart
Copyright © 1986 by Susan C. Feldhake

Reprinted as Book Two of the Enduring Faith Series in 1993

Requests for information should be addressed to:
Zondervan Publishing House
Grand Rapids, Michigan 49530

Library of Congress Cataloging in Publication Data

Feldhake, Susan C.
   Seasons of the heart / Susan C. Feldhake.
     p.   cm. – (Enduring faith series : bk. 2)
   ISBN 0-310-48121-X
   I. Title. II. Series: Feldhake, Susan C. Enduring faith series : bk. 2.
PS3556.E4575S4   1993
813'.54—dc20   92-33215
                                       CIP

Edited by Anne Severance
Cover design by Jody Langley
Illustrations by Bob Sabin

Printed in the United States of America

95 96 97 98 99 00 01 02 / DH / 13 12 11 10 9 8 7 6 5 4

For my editors,
Anne Severance,
Bob Hudson,
and Sandra Vander Zicht,
with warmest wishes
and much appreciation
for their combined efforts
and individual encouragement.

And for all the wonderful readers
who wanted to know
"what happened next"
—my enduring thanks!

Prologue
April 1873

ALTON WHEELER caressed the costly green ribbon, recalling
the emotions that had welled in him one year ago and
remained with him yet on this—his wedding day.

The feelings had arrived then so unexpectedly and without
warrant that Alton had been moved to purchase the brilliant
scrap of fabric at the notions counter in the general store in
Effingham, Illinois. The color matched perfectly the emerald
eyes of Sue Ellen Stone, the woman he had almost killed on
that bright April day!

His mind lingered on that precipitous meeting, when Sue
Ellen had stepped into the path of his wagon, unintentionally
altering the course of his life. Helplessly Alton's thoughts
spun back over the seasons.

That day Alton's head had been throbbing, his tongue, thick
as quilt batting, and his stomach, queasily rebelling at every
bump in the road.

Alton sighed with discontent, inhaling the suffocating dust
churned up by Doc's and Dan's hooves as they clopped over
the rough trails, cleaving the prairies to connect the burgeon-
ing communities that had sprung up as the nation's citizens
trekked westward.

His wagon lumbered into the Effingham County seat just as a train noisily departed. Lethargic from the heat and his inebriated state, Alton gave little thought to the direction his wanderings would take. He loosened his grip on the reins, giving the team their heads. They could choose with as much surety as he!

The large grays—matched Clydesdales, a stallion and a gelding, won in a recent blackjack game with a German farmer near St. Louis, Missouri—had thundered toward the left, the route that would cause Alton's life to collide tumultuously with that of Sue Ellen Stone.

Even in his drowsy state, he *had* noticed her—a pretty mite of a thing, wearing widow's weeds and the sad expression of a lost child.

As the horses barreled down the red brick road, Alton assumed that the widow woman had safely crossed the street, but when he glanced in her direction, Alton discovered that she had not moved out of his way at all! Indeed, she seemed bent on approach!

Horrified, he stared down at her, pale and slight, dwarfed by the massive Clydesdales bearing down on her.

"Whoa!"

With a frenzied cry Alton leaped to his feet and desperately hauled on the reins, hardly daring to hope that the horses' footing would hold on the bricks worn smooth, their color dulled by a skim of dust.

Awareness entered the woman's features an instant before the rig reached her, and Alton knew he would forever be haunted by the gentle, startled face that looked up to his in mutual recognition of the danger. Then the stampeding beasts blocked the widow from view, and the wagon bucked ahead.

Alton willed his ears not to hear the shrill screams, nor his

8

body to acknowledge the thump and jolt as the woman was flung under the high wooden wagon wheels like a rag doll.

But he heard nothing, felt nothing.

Only when the wagon clattered by, leaving the faded skirt of the widow's black gown unclaimed by the spinning spokes that had greedily sucked at the billowing fabric, did he allow himself to believe that she had escaped what appeared to be certain death.

Glancing over his shoulder at the woman, untouched and unharmed, he felt the draining relief deep within. So relieved was Alton Wheeler, in fact, that he reacted with grateful fury. As the newly unfurling maple leaves whispered overhead and the swaying branches creaked and moaned, Alton bellowed with rage until he was void of further speech or action.

The widow's oval face grew as pale as her dress was dark.

Alton had believed himself spent of emotion until he saw the sheen of her unshed tears. He stood mute, an unwilling witness to her misery as one convicting drop fell from a long black lash.

Then Alton glanced down the tracks and, noticing what must be the widow's young son seated on a large trunk, felt a surge of regret that spiraled to an unbearable height. The youth had observed the entire shameful scene—his mother near death, this giant of a stranger railing at her like a man possessed instead of offering her his courteous protection.

He'd been raised better than that! Alton's thoughts flew back to his early years when, even though his pa was dead, his mother, God bless her, had raised him to know right from wrong. He couldn't continue on his way without at least the offer of an apology.

Stammering and flushing, Alton forced the difficult words to find the path leading from mind to tongue. When the widow responded with a forgiving smile, Alton suddenly felt an apology wasn't enough; a good deed was in order! Before he knew it, the tall wagonmaster found himself agreeing to Widow Stone's plea that he hire out for the day and haul them—herself and her son—to their new home, a farm on Salt Creek.

Even as he made the transaction, Alton felt an unreasonable urge to turn and run, leaving the defenseless widow to tend to her child the way a pitiful old barn tabby might care for a lone kitten.

But he couldn't do it. There was something about the woman that compelled him to follow through on his agreement. In the telling, her problems had become his to share, his to solve. And this he proceeded to do, his mind crawling over and examining the obstacles she and the boy might face when he left them on the piece of land they had journeyed from Minnesota to claim.

Mindful of her finances, at the general store Alton had selected tools, equipment, and items necessary to eke out their existence. Only when he was through making his selection did Alton turn to summon Widow Stone to the counter to pay the bill, and as he did, he saw her fingering the expensive green ribbon, yearning in her eyes. He saw, too, the discipline she exerted to withhold purchase of the gewgaw, even though the frayed black ribbons now binding her hair would soon become tattered beyond use.

Not knowing if it was the decent thing to do, scarcely caring if it wasn't, Alton slipped back into the store and surreptitiously purchased the ribbon. He would drop the fabric somewhere so that it would be found, or tuck the delicate finery amongst the family's possessions to be later discovered like an unexpected treasure, accepted and enjoyed, if only because he wasn't present to suffer its refusal and return.

A violent summer storm passed and darkness draped the area before Alton had borne the widow and her son to their farm. Alton knew that he should be on his way but couldn't bring himself to abandon this woman who produced such a wealth of emotion in him. So he lingered on, announcing that he wanted to be sure the property was fit and safe before he took his leave.

Already, with an acquaintanceship measured in mere hours, Alton was shaken by the truth that the widow could tip his world upside down with a shy smile, or, with the hint of a frown, send his thoughts skittering backward to find and correct possible offense. Believing himself a worldly man capable of facing whatever came his way, Alton realized he hadn't felt such a seesaw of emotions since he was in kneepants.

Alton was further disturbed by the unsettling sensation that somehow all that he'd learned about women over the years did not apply to this good, God-fearing widow who treated him as if he were somebody.

In truth, he hadn't known who he was. Orphaned as a child, with no permanent place to call home, for most of his life Alton had drifted from town to town. He'd made his livelihood as he could—taking the place of a rich young man who paid him to perform in his stead during the Civil War, manning the barges on the mighty Mississippi, and, of late, trusting his future to the flip of a card in a saloon, where the stench of stale cigar smoke competed with the cheap perfume of the barroom girls.

How could it be, then, that this place, this woman and her son, this life, felt like the *home* he'd never really known? And how could an existence so unrelated to any he'd ever lived before hold such appeal, and, instinctively, feel so . . . right?

By all rights, Alton knew that he ought to be moving on,

even as he searched for reasons to stay if only for a brief spell. Darkness would stay his departure until morning. But then he would have no cause not to set out, leaving behind a part of his heart.

That night, wrapped in a bright quilt Sue Ellen had given him in addition to payment and sheltered in the barn while Doc and Dan pastured in the meadow, Alton was restless. For the first time since childhood he found himself praying, hoping for the answers that would allow him to stay near this remarkable woman.

Thunder crashed to cleave the sky.

Lightning flared with brilliant promise.

Sluicing rain pelted the earth, washing away Alton's cares and worries, as water rushed from the hillsides, collected in the valley, and for days thereafter, barred passage through the flooded creek until soon neither he nor Sue Ellen Stone spoke again of his leaving.

Ah, the rich seasons of the heart, Alton thought, as he watched Sue Ellen twine the green fabric through her dark curls, fulfilling his promise given nine months before, that his bride would have emerald ribbons in her hair.

There is a season for all things—love, too—he mused. Their love had budded in April, bloomed in June, then wilted in July, seared by his fiery fury when she'd refused his proposal of marriage.

Even with his wedding day at hand and the ceremony moments away, Alton's heart squeezed with the hurtful memory. He had planned the declaration of his love so carefully! Why, his hope and surety had known no bounds after Sue Ellen had kissed him as fervently as she had—the way no woman would kiss a man whom she didn't want above all others.

He'd stammered his humble proposal with vulnerable certainty that she would take him, loving her as he did. But Sue Ellen had cast his offer of marriage aside, told him she couldn't marry him because he was not a Christian man. . . .

The rage he'd felt in the face of this cruel rejection knew no bounds. He had said things that no woman could truly ever forgive—no woman, that is, but Sue Ellen Stone.

And then he had fled.

Late summer found him back in saloons, familiar places, but no longer appealing after the wholesome fun of the Salt Creek neighbors' pie socials and barn raisings. Indian summer was warm with friendship and growing self-worth as he began to live, not by the turn of the card, but by the sweat of his brow. Winter's bitterness was intensified with loneliness, longing, and the tormenting notion that perhaps Sue Ellen had wed another. And then came spring and the dawning of faith—a fresh beginning.

Hope was born anew for Alton with the discovery that true love is eternal in its origin and that, in God's own time, a man and a woman who trust in Him can weather the changing seasons of the heart, their steadfast love bearing fruit at last.

The springtime of their love was in the past, Alton realized, his pulse quickening with anticipation. Now he would reach out with Sue Ellen to harvest the fragrant blossoms of happiness tended in their summer years to preserve as precious memories to feast upon in the autumn of their lives.

I
Sue Ellen

chapter
1

ALTON WHEELER felt a ripple of weakness wash over him. He could not decide if the dizzying sensation was the lingering effect of the rattlesnake bite suffered the day before, or the heady realization that in a few short minutes the pastor would arrive and Sue Ellen Stone would become his bride.

Sensing his gaze on her, Sue Ellen turned and confronted his smile with a grin of her own. She looked so appealing that he ached to sweep her into his arms and steal one last kiss before the ceremony. But before he could make a move, Sue Ellen cocked her head, listening.

The gentle breeze that seemed to stir perpetually over the hilly Illinois region, whatever the season, tugged playfully at the crisp ribbons and hopscotched through the curly dark tresses that tickled Sue Ellen's smooth, pink cheeks. A joyous glint gave light to her sparkling eyes and she impulsively fit her hand into Alton's.

"Listen!" she cried. "They're almost here!"

Faintly resonant, the steady clip-clop of hooves echoed on the hard-packed clay trail that wound its way through hills and hollows to the Stone farm on the banks of Salt Creek.

For a moment it seemed almost impossible to Alton that only the day before he had traversed the narrow, winding trail himself, with Doc and Dan eagerly conquering the rolling terrain, as he returned to claim the woman chosen for him by God.

Sue Ellen's hand tightened on his, and Alton knew that he would never leave her again. *Never!*

"There they are!" she breathed happily.

Hand in hand, they crossed the lawn. Sue Ellen stood on tiptoe to peer over the budding blackberry briars and the wild roses intertwined on the split-rail fence that flanked the lane leading to the snug homestead.

"The preacher's here, Sue!" Alton pointed. "And there's Will and Fanny Preston, too!"

Pastor Clark's somber black carriage, drawn by a sorrel mare, bobbed as it negotiated the turn. To the rear of the carriage rode Jem, perched on Doc's broad back. Craggy-faced, lean Will Preston, his hair whiter than Alton had remembered, sat astride a brown saddle horse. Plump, ginger-haired Fanchon Preston—known as Fanny throughout the neighborhood—had squeezed her girth into the carriage beside the congenial, black-clothed clergyman.

"Whoa!" Jem bawled at Doc, sawing on the reins.

The smiling preacher tipped his hat in Sue Ellen's direction and reined in the sorrel. The horse came to a halt, snorting, and then shook its mane, setting the harness hardware to jingling.

"Howdy!" Will cried, grinning.

Calling out his greeting, Pastor Clark wrapped the reins around the carriage brake and climbed stiffly out of the conveyance, before turning back to assist Fanny to solid ground. Will had already dismounted and stood by to take his jolly wife's other hand. The high-wheeled carriage swayed then dipped precariously, causing Fanny to giggle and gasp.

18

She held her breath as her tiny feet sought the metal steps descending from the carriage.

"Welcome home, Alton!" Will boomed. "Good to have you back in the community, my man! And, this time . . . to stay."

Alton accepted the friendly grip. "Mighty glad to be back, Will," Alton admitted. "Your farm was lookin' good when I passed by yesterday. I noticed your new foals. They're dandies."

Will nodded proudly. "Right nice horseflesh," he agreed, and laid a gnarled hand across Doc's broad rump as Jem led the horses toward the water trough in the pasture. "That stallion of yours sired some fine foals." Will gave a cackle. "Reckon I'm about as glad to see Dan in the neighborhood as I am *you!*"

Glancing pointedly at the minister, Fanny flushed and nudged Will, with a silent admonition to leave the subject of livestock and their reproduction.

"Fanny, I'm so glad you and Will are here to serve as witnesses!" Sue Ellen returned the plump woman's crushing hug.

Beaming, Fanny patted Sue Ellen affectionately and lowered her voice to a conspiratorial whisper. "I declare! I've waited for this day so long that you know I wouldn't miss it for the world," she said. "'Twas like a miracle—'twas a miracle of answered prayer—when Jem dropped by on the way to the preacher and told us there was goin' to be a weddin'."

Will harumphed and adjusted his hat, squinting as he eyed Alton's arm where the bandage bulged beneath his shirt. "Feared for a moment it was going to be a buryin', Al," Will said. "Jem told us about the accident in the woods yesterday. Rattlesnakes can be right testy this time of year. You're made of stout stuff to be up an' around so soon."

19

"Thanks to Sue, I'm doin' just fine," Alton acknowledged, slipping his arm around her slim waist.

Sue Ellen gently squeezed his forearm. "Thanks to the *Lord,* you'll be fine," she corrected.

Alton tenderly laid his hand over hers. "Whatever you say," he agreed, catching the wink that Will cast in his direction.

"What do you say we have a wedding?" Pastor Clark suggested. "The lilac hedge would make a pleasant setting."

"Perfect!" Fanny agreed. Taking two steps to Sue Ellen's one, they strolled toward the flowery bower. "You're a picture in that dress, honey," she said, admiring the delicate silk gown with its fine green floral print against a white background. The full skirt, ruffled hem, scooped neckline, and short puffed sleeves further complemented Sue Ellen's beauty.

"Thank you, Fanny. You're sweet to say so."

"Now aren't you glad that a year ago Alton stopped you before you tore up that gown to make curtains for the cabin? It's the perfect marryin' dress," Fanny puffed, panting with exertion. "Not that it's the gown that makes you beautiful, although granted, it does play a part. 'Tis the love in your eyes and fillin' your heart that adorns you best, Sue Ellen Stone."

"That it does," Will agreed, falling into step beside his wife and cupping her elbow to steady her progress over the rough sod. "I don't believe you've ever looked purtier, Sue."

"The radiance brought by love for a good, Christian man," Fanny sighed, as she cast Alton an affectionate glance. "And what joy it gives my old heart to pass that judgment, Alton, you rascal!" she teased, and shook her finger at him. "You've given us much concern these past months, you handsome scamp! But, 'tis easy to forgive you because your return represents the answer to a good many prayers, what with you standin' here big as life and us about to witness you takin' Sue Ellen to wed!"

20

"It's good to be back amongst you, Fanny. With Sue Ellen, with Jem—with all of you."

Fanny settled herself on a smooth spot on the lawn, and Will positioned himself beside her.

"I had nary a doubt that you'd be back," Fanny admitted stoutly. She chewed her lower lip and shook her head sadly. "But, poor Sue! She was heartbroke! I knew you'd be back in love's own time, as I reminded Sue many a day."

"Oh, Fanny—hush!" Sue Ellen cried, blushing.

"Shush your protests, gal!" Fanny retorted good-naturedly. "It's good for your man to know that you were as heartsick and filled with longin' as he."

Jem arrived, slicked his fingers through his hair, and stood erect. Pastor Clark glanced at him with welcome relief, consulted his pocket watch, then cleared his throat.

"Shall we begin?"

Sue Ellen and Alton exchanged a nervous glance, then joined hands before the minister. Fanny folded her arms across her stout figure and settled back on her heels, prepared to savor the long-awaited moment. Will presented his good ear to the pastor, the better to catch the melodic words that quickly wafted away on the gentle wind.

"Dearly beloved . . . ," Pastor Clark began. "We are gathered here today . . ."

To Alton, these were the most beautiful words in the language, delivered with a poetic cadence, as the preacher's rich voice rose and fell in the emotion of describing scripturally the mysteries of love.

Alton stole a glance at Sue Ellen's pure profile and noticed that she was clinging to the words as intently as he. Her hand in his trembled, and with difficulty he tore his gaze away from her radiant face.

But Alton was so overwhelmed with happiness that he

could scarcely follow the words of the ceremony. His thoughts flooded forth, moving like turbulent, bubbling white water that carried him rapidly toward an eddying whirlpool of memories in which he felt himself drowning in the realization of Sue Ellen's abiding love for him.

Alton had no idea that he was grinning like a fool until he caught Jem's amused smile. With a sheepish start he stood erect, embarrassed by the realization of the figure he was cutting in this solemn moment. Alton cleared his throat, shifted his feet, and valiantly fought to focus on the pastor's words as he began to guide Sue Ellen through the sacred vows she offered before God.

The honeyed tones of her voice, however, made concentration that much more difficult as Alton recalled other words, other times when she'd confessed her love for him. Those willful, blurted admissions had been all that had sustained him during their long separation, all that had fostered his helpless desire to believe that she might be waiting for him.

Alton was so ensnared by his memories that a long moment passed before he became aware of the sudden expectant silence surrounding them.

"Do you take this woman as your lawfully wedded wife? To have and to hold? In sickness and in health? Forsaking all others, until death do you part?" the pastor prompted, repeating the questions he had posed only a moment before.

Alton jerked to attention. "Oh, my heavens, yes! 'Course I do!"

Will and Jem exchanged amused glances as Pastor Clark proceeded with the ceremony. Alton had no further time for woolgathering about his good fortune. An instant later, Pastor Clark declared Sue Ellen his wife before God and man, and Alton closed his eyes in thankful prayer.

"You may kiss the bride," the pastor invited.

Alton opened his eyes to confront the happy gazes of these people who were so dear to him—Fanny, Will, Jem. He met their eyes as if seeking their permission to approach the woman he so cherished.

With a soft smile, Sue Ellen lifted her shining eyes to his. He knew that the woman who had always understood him so well seemed to understand this hesitancy, too. Alton's heart ached with love as she slipped her slim arms around his neck and stood on tiptoe that their lips might meet.

"I love you," Sue Ellen whispered against Alton's warm mouth. "I love you now and forever. . . ."

Time stood still.

Alton was aware of nothing except the sweet, yielding pliancy of Sue Ellen's lips surrendering to his.

A flurry of hugs and congratulations followed.

With dispatch the preacher completed the formalities, showing Will and Fanny where to add their signatures to the marriage document. Then, shaking hands all around, he took his leave, with Alton's thanks and a gold coin for his trouble.

Pastor Clark had scarcely departed when neighbors began to arrive. Nickering horses, gay laughter, and the creaking thunk of wagon wheels on the rutted road heralded their approach. Fanny grinned when the sight drew puzzled looks from Alton and Sue Ellen.

"We knew the neighbors shouldn't be denied the chance for a git-together," she explained. "When Jem stopped by to ask Will 'n' me to witness the weddin', Will sent Rory skedaddlin' to put out word in the neighborhood to meet here for a social."

"It appears they're *all* turnin' out," Alton said, dazed.

"Of course they are!" Fanny agreed in a hearty tone. "Why not? We're all your friends. They're plumb tickled to have you back, Al."

A continuous stream of neighbors paraded up the lane. They came in battered carriages, on weather-beaten buckboards, clinging to high-walled farm wagons, and on horseback, with one and all dressed in their Sunday best.

The men grinned and nodded, quietly offering Alton words of welcome and congratulations as they filed by, tipping their hats to Sue Ellen. The women winked at Sue and hid giggles of delight behind reddened, work-chapped hands. Craning their necks to survey the jumble of wagons, they waggled fingers at other neighborhood women present with their lively broods.

The farmers lined up their rigs and slipped feedbags in place over the velvety noses of their horses and mules, then helped their wives with the hampers and baskets of food as children tumbled from the wagons, spilling to the ground amid shrieks of laughter.

Fanny and Will took charge of the feast. Under their direction a plank table was quickly erected. Bright cloths were whisked into place. Soon the improvised banquet table fairly groaned beneath the weight of dishes intended for evening meals and supplemented with delicacies and cakes put by for the occasion.

Late afternoon gave way to twilight and then to full darkness, and rambunctious youngsters, weary of play, crept closer to the bonfire Jem had built to discourage mosquitoes and provide light for the neighbors' visiting. The grown folks talked in hushed tones as the smaller children climbed onto their fathers' laps and tiny babes slumbered at their mothers' breasts.

With a show of reluctance the congenial group at last acknowledged the lateness of the hour, gathered their belongings, and tucked blankets around their sleeping little ones for the leisurely ride home.

The men lit lanterns, exchanged final greetings, took their places behind the reins, and, one by one, the wagons rolled out as the horses stomped and snorted their impatience to be off.

"You all come back, hear?" Alton called after them. "Thanks for droppin' by!"

"Wouldn't have missed it!"

"Come see us, too!"

"Welcome back, Alton!"

"Congratulations, you two!"

Alton and Sue Ellen stood beneath the towering oak tree and watched the departure of these good people, good friends all. Soon the carriage lanterns were but glowing dots winking in the darkness, gradually merging with the flare of fireflies flitting through the night.

Jem yawned openly. Alton stifled his own.

"Well, I'm going to turn in," Jem said, yawning again. "Good-night, Mama. Good-night, Alton . . . Pa."

"G'night . . . son," Alton murmured and watched him go.

Sue Ellen sighed and tucked a stray wisp of hair behind her ear. "What a wonderful day," she whispered. Alton slipped his arms around her and the warmth of his hands encountered her cool skin. Sue Ellen shivered, he knew not if from his touch or from the moist chill of the night air.

"Cool?" he asked.

She shook her head. "Just tired. It's time to go to bed, Alton," she said, brushing his cheek with the flat of her palm as she slipped from the circle of his arms. She tucked her hand into his, her soft, round shoulder coming to rest against his bare forearm.

The close contact jarred Alton to full wakefulness. The moment of their union was at hand, draining him of confidence and making him hollow with insecurity. Feeling

25

almost ill, he longed for the return of the neighbors, the continuation of revelry, protection against the approaching intimacies he both feared and desired with all his being.

His heart thundered, yet he remained rooted as solidly as the massive oak tree less than an arm's length away. Numb, Alton watched Jem move through the darkness across the lush lawn to duck into the snug cabin. He knew the boy would be feeling his way through the familiar rooms until he came to the crude ladder, would cover the distance in two or three long steps, then would light the oil lantern in his room under the rafters. Alton waited for the lamp to flare, signaling that Jem was readying himself for bed.

Moments later the light was snuffed out, and Alton tried to produce the courage required to take the few steps across the knoll and into the cabin. But for Alton, it was like crossing a deep, wide chasm from which there was no return. He hated the sinking sensations that stole his strength away and left the coppery taste of fright on his tongue. Suddenly the unknown awaiting him in Sue Ellen's bed was more fearsome than any terrors entertained in the dark bowels of the coal mine, that special place of torment where he had lost his best friend, Tom McPherson, but had gained total trust in and commitment to the Lord.

Oh . . . dear God . . . Alton's heart cried out now for strength and guidance.

"Come, Alton," Sue Ellen whispered. "It's time to turn in."

Like a sleepwalker Alton followed Sue Ellen into the dark cabin. Their whispers, echoing in the stillness, seemed to crash like thunder.

Sue Ellen produced matches and a coal oil lamp. She touched the flame to the wick, and a comforting glow sprang up to be magnified within the globe. After securing the chimney, Sue Ellen gripped the ornate handle and led the way to her neat, small bedroom.

Alton remained near the hearth, motionless as a boulder. Conflicting emotions warred within him. In contemplation of the coming moments, cold sweat popped out on his forehead. Trapped, he wallowed in bewilderment that left him almost strangling with rage at his own stupidity. How did one proceed with a good, decent woman . . . a Christian wife . . . an angel like Sue Ellen?

If only he knew what to do, how to behave, Alton silently lamented.

Tom McPherson, who'd died for him in the mine, had been a Christian man, married to a woman of faith. Oh, why hadn't he wangled a general idea of such things out of Tom when he'd had the chance? Alton realized, too late, that he might have found a way to broach the subject delicately. Tom, who was always guided by the Word of God, would have been glad enough to instruct him in the godly way to approach matters of intimate human conduct.

Alton felt numb with indecision. He loved Sue Ellen so dearly that it would be a pain worse than death to consider hurting, offending, disappointing, or somehow humiliating her in any way. What if, out of ignorance, he trampled her modesty in a stampede of unrestrainable desire and forever damaged his standing in her eyes?

"Alton?" Sue Ellen called, a hint of worry in her tone.

Alton's response was a tormented sigh. He gouged his arm against the mantelpiece to provide momentum to begin his journey to Sue Ellen's—*their*—bedroom. En route, he massaged his eyes and kneaded the vein at his temple, which had begun to pound with tension and the traitorous thought that, just for tonight, he wished Sue Ellen Stone Wheeler

27

were one of those cheerful, pleasant bawdy ladies that a man needn't worry about offending.

At least then, Alton thought in dogged pursuit of the logic, he'd know how to predict her reaction. Although he was not proud of the fact, in the past he'd had occasional encounters with flashy women of the night. With so little to lose—only a few coins, and them easily replaced—he'd been supremely confident. But as a husband, how could he tolerate the crippling knowledge that his cherished wife might despise and despair of him for proceeding with her in the only way he knew?

As Alton's feet carried him to the portal of the bedroom, he saw the room he would share with Sue Ellen—quaint, neatly furnished, bathed in the golden, welcoming glow of the lamp perched high on a shelf above the cot. To his glance, Sue Ellen seemed unaware of his utter confusion as she readied the room, turned down the covers, and brushed her dark hair until it gleamed and hung loose around her slim shoulders. She was encased, head to toe, in a crisp, modest cotton nightdress.

Alton stood like a centurion as she seated herself on the straw tick, the ropes affixed to the frame swinging rhythmically. Sue Ellen smiled up at him as she brushed her hair. Swallowing hard, Alton licked his lips and glanced away. The cotton gown did little to conceal the fact that Sue Ellen was a beautiful, appealing woman.

"Come to bed, Alton. You're not a well man. You need your rest."

Rest!

Alton's thoughts dived for, and clung to, the directive hidden in her speech. Surely it was a ladylike, well-bred, genteel hint that Sue Ellen expected nothing—desired nothing—in the way of husbandly attention this night.

28

Evading Sue Ellen's gaze, Alton crossed the room that suddenly seemed entirely too small for his large frame. Woodenly he blew out the lantern, plunging the room into protective, comforting darkness.

Only then did Alton dare seat himself on the opposite edge of the swaying mattress. The straw crackled and the ropes whined beneath his weight as he removed his boots.

Scarcely able to breathe because of the knot constricting his chest, Alton picked at the buttons on his shirt. His ragged breathing seemed to be magnified a hundredfold. Sue Ellen said nothing, waiting in silence, making the simple noises of his undressing seem unduly loud. One by one, his garments hit the smooth floor, since in the dark he could not decide where else to deposit them.

Tense as coiled steel, Alton eased back on the starched, freshly laundered pillowslip. He lay rigid, afraid to breathe, fearful of movement, praying that somehow this wedding night would pass.

Alton lay as one dead, fearful that his skin would accidentally brush against Sue Ellen's silken form. No matter how stoutly he tried to banish them, tormenting visions raced through his mind, filling him with longing for the beloved woman beside him, while the still, humid night wrapped him in velvety warmth.

Long minutes passed.

From the pattern of her breathing, Alton knew that Sue Ellen was not asleep, either. Perhaps they could talk, relive the moments of the day until he could still his rapid heartbeat, regain a dram of manly confidence. But his mind gave no assistance.

Moths beat against the screen. Through the open window, he could hear insects of the night, humming and rasping. In the pasture beyond, Doc and Dan nickered, reminding him of those nights a year ago when he had bedded down in the stable with only his horses for company. Again the animals whinnied, beckoning him, it seemed. He bolted upright, grateful for this means of escape from the suffocating confinement of his own heart.

"I . . . I think I'd better go check on the horses," Alton muttered his excuse, swinging his feet to the floor. Mortified by the way in which the words sounded on his lips, he was even more confounded by the sound of Sue Ellen's laughter!

As he struggled to counter the rebellious swinging of the bedropes supporting the crackling straw tick that flung him backward each time he leaned forward, Sue Ellen's restraining hand sought him. Her soft chuckle wrapped around him like a protective embrace.

"Alton . . . oh my dear, beloved Alton," Sue Ellen whispered. Her voice, lilting with love and rich with understanding, was spiced with coquettish amusement. "Doc and Dan are fine—just fine. It's *you* who's skittish as a colt. From this day forward, Alton, your place isn't out in the stable with your horses. Your rightful place is beside me. Don't leave me now. Don't leave me—ever!"

"Sue . . . I . . . uh . . ."

Alton groped for words of explanation—words that stubbornly refused to submit to his lips. A moment later he realized there was no need. Just as Sue Ellen had understood him so well and fully in the past, she did not fail him now, as his wife.

Her arms slipped boldly around him and her kiss branded him with her love. Her soft encouragement was his joyous command, and he knew that she shared his awe, his thanksgiving, his delight in their union that joined them in body, mind, and spirit—one, forever.

Never had a moment seemed so right, so decent, so good,

than this private promise of commitment, faith, and love that made their vows of the afternoon a sacred troth deeper than any pledge Alton had ever before given. His spirit soared as he gave and accepted that joyful adoration that only each could bestow on the other—the perfect wedding gift created by God.

Long after Sue Ellen had fallen asleep in his arms, her breath soft as a newborn babe's against his shoulder, Alton lay awake, smiling into the darkness.

Helplessly he shook his head over the dizzying aspects of true love. Then he was overcome with gratitude to the Lord for selecting a woman like Sue Ellen as the perfect helpmate for him. His heart offered a prayer of thanksgiving, before adding one more humble, heartfelt request—that he might never disappoint this woman nor betray the Lord's confidence in leading him back to her. Never.

chapter
2

ALTON SHIFTED in his sleep, wincing when he rolled over, and the bandage bit into his arm. Quickly sleep abandoned him. Alton flipped his eyes open and, before he could turn his face to Sue Ellen's pillow, which still bore the indentation of her head, he knew that the room felt devoid of her presence.

When he remembered the forthright, passionate woman he'd come to know as his wife the night before, he quickly dressed and entered the kitchen, feeling suddenly shy. Upon seeing her, prim and modest, he might have categorized the shadowy remembrances of the night before as some kind of teasing torment, except that in Sue Ellen's eyes, he saw the glow of love well fulfilled.

She inquired about his arm, possessively patting his shoulder as she bade him be seated at the table to enjoy a cup of coffee while she prepared the morning meal. Then she set about her task efficiently. Again, he wondered at this woman he had married—her hair coiled tightly at the nape of her neck—hiding the very different one who had taken out the pins last night to envelop them in a raven cloud.

"I'll have sausage and flapjacks ready in a wink," Sue Ellen promised. "And lots of maple syrup. I remember how you love it!"

Alton patted his stomach, then lifted his coffee mug, taking a sip of the scalding brew. "Ain't had a flapjack as light as yours since the day I left," he commented. "Where's Jem?"

"He should be returning from checking the trot lines shortly. He's been up since dawn."

"Jem's become a fine young man since last I saw 'im," Alton said reflectively.

Sue Ellen smiled to herself and cracked an egg into the bowl of flour. "You gave him good example before you left."

Almost as if their words were a cue, the youth entered the snug kitchen. Jem washed his hands in the basin, dashed water over his face and through his hair, dried himself, then took a seat across from Alton.

"G' mornin', Pa," he said. "Sure is a pretty day."

"That it is, son," Alton said. "It appears we'll have fit weather for workin' the soil. What plans might you have fer the day?"

"Nothing special," Jem answered. He explained that he'd been tending to early spring chores, preparing to plant the corn crop needed to feed the animals. "I'll welcome your help where you can assist, Pa, but I expect you'll tire fast for a while. Thank the good Lord, that snake bite was no worse than it was."

"We've got a lot to be thankful for," Sue Ellen chimed in. "It seems as if we've had a whole year's worth of blessings rolled up into scarcely more than a day."

She placed platters of food on the table, then seated herself and folded her hands before glancing expectantly at Alton. "Would you honor us by asking the blessing?"

Alton clasped his large, rough hands together. Suddenly overcome by a realization of the bountiful blessings so richly bestowed even when his faith had been impoverished, Alton felt incapable of expressing his appreciation to such a patient, loving, generous Lord. He sat for a full minute without uttering a word over the lump in his throat. Then, like a log jam unbinding, the words began to flow and his gratitude knew no bounds.

"Amen," Sue Ellen and Jeremiah spoke in unison at the end of his eloquent thanksgiving.

That day, as Jem had predicted, Alton tired easily, and the next, as well. But even in his weakened state, he found plenty he could do around the hilly forty-acre farm, and as one day was replaced by the next, Alton's arm mended and his full strength returned.

Alton and the workhorses plowed and harrowed the fields. Jem and Sue Ellen planted the corn. A week later tiny chartreuse shoots split the earth.

Under Sue Ellen's direction, Alton and Jem set out delicate vegetable plants, buried hills of seeds, and mounded soil over tubers, with faith that their careful tending would provide them with food to see them through the long winter months.

That summer, when time allowed, Alton spaded beds for Sue Ellen's flowers, arranging a special surprise when he and Jeremiah transplanted wild roses from the woods to form a pleasant rock garden near the cabin. There was even a rough bench built from split logs, so that she might sit and seek a rare moment of rest from her busy workday.

It was there that Alton found her one June day, pale and wan, when he returned from the woods. When she had not immediately responded to his call, sudden fear had struck to the core of his being and he had bolted from the ominously still cabin, bellowing Sue Ellen's name over and over.

Finally he heard her reply—a frail, almost inaudible bleat. Unable to discern the direction from which her cry had come, he looked high and low, fearing the worst.

Weakly she called out again.

Alton sprinted toward the rock garden and found her

slumped on the bench, her eyes glassy, her body racked with spasms. Turning away, she pressed a white handkerchief to her pale lips. When Alton spoke her name, she regarded him with misery in her green eyes until yet another spasm of nausea gripped her.

"Sue! Sue! Sh—should I send Jem fer the doctor?" he cried, his voice reedy with fright. "Are you going to be all right? Answer me, woman!"

Inching the handkerchief from her lips, as if testing to see if she dared, Sue Ellen's eyelids slipped shut and she tilted her head back and drew a deep breath, smoothing the tangled hair from her face.

"Yes . . . no . . . I mean . . . yes," she sighed. "I'm all right. I . . . I'll *be* all right," she breathed the words. "There's no use sending for a doctor yet, Alton. Later." She gave him a faltering smile. "There's nothing he can do for me . . . now."

Alton was unconvinced. A deep frown etched his features. "You're sure you'll be all right, Sue? It ain't like you to be sickly this way."

Sue Ellen stared at the ground. "Perhaps because I haven't been sick . . . this way . . . in quite a spell, Alton. It just took me all of the sudden. I'd all but forgotten what it's like to be . . . in the family way. It's been fourteen years."

Alton's mouth dropped open. "Y—you're going to bear us a little 'un?" he gasped.

With her nod, it seemed as if a thousand emotions— strong, intense, conflicting—welled within him.

"Come the New Year, we'll have a new babe," Sue Ellen calmly announced.

"Oh, Sue . . ."

Further speech failed Alton. Sue Ellen arose and took his arm, steadying herself. From habit, he slipped his arm around her and she leaned against him.

"I hope you're not upset," Sue Ellen whispered. "I . . . I've been praying that it'd happen. I'm so happy—please don't be disappointed."

"Disappointed?" Alton cried, aghast, giving her a quick, affirming hug. "Why, this seems 'bout the most wonderful thing that could happen to a feller when the woman he loves presents him with a little 'un."

"I'm so glad you're happy," Sue Ellen said, her voice gaining strength with the relief.

Even as Alton held Sue Ellen close, his mind wandered, skittering hither and yon as his plans and attention exploded in all directions at once. His dreams were soft utterances, spoken at the moment of their conception.

"I'll build a cradle—stout as you please, but pleasin' to the eye, as well—" He paused. "I reckon I'd better build you more shelves in the cellar, too—what with another mouth to feed—" Suddenly Alton halted in his rambling. He gave Sue Ellen a hug and kissed the tip of her nose. "Why, as much as there is to do, I'll be a busy man till the end of December!"

"No doubt that's why the Lord gives a period of waiting before a birthing," murmured Sue Ellen, "so there's plenty of time to ready the home and heart to receive the little one He's sending. I'll have to get some yard goods—soft flannel—to stitch into small garments. And some pretty quilts and coverlets." Sue Ellen shivered, then hugged herself as she preceded Alton into the cabin. "Oh, Alton, I'm so happy I'm almost afraid. It's like I've possessed heaven and all that it offers, here on earth. Oh, just pray that nothing can dim the happiness we know now!"

At her words a chill of dread knifed through Alton. How many times, already, had he awakened in the night, drenched in a cold sweat, his heart hammering, his mind wild until he'd reached out and touched Sue Ellen's serene form, thus reassuring himself that happiness was still within his grasp.

"Nothin' will happen, Sue darlin'," Alton told her, with more confidence than he felt. "We won't let it!"

As Alton held Sue Ellen—the woman who encompassed and inspired his happiness—fear snaked through his being, striking out with venomous rationale. Suddenly his fear intensified.

What if it all ended? How would he bear it?

With growing horror Alton recalled how Tom McPherson, a Christian, God-fearing man, if ever there was one, had known such happiness, too. And how Tommy had suffered! He'd borne being parted from his dear wife, Sadie, for weeks at a time so he could labor in the dank depths of the coal mine to provide for the family's needs. Then word had come that his child—his precious little girl, Mandy—was dead of the cholera. Tom accepted it with a quiet faith that had scalded Alton's unbelieving soul.

But Alton knew that Tom could bear anything. Even death. Helplessly, Alton examined himself—recognized his weaknesses, admitted his doubts. More than once tragedy had struck Tom McPherson, who was a better man than he, by far, and he had borne it all without bitterness to the day of his own untimely death. But Alton didn't know how he could survive if something happened to Sue or to their unborn child. Would hard times wreck their love and happiness—or make them stronger? Alton wondered if his still fragile faith was the kind that could take anything the future might hold—hurt, disappointment, death—and turn it into praise for the God who could bring good from it.

"Don't frown so, Alton Wheeler!" Sue Ellen chided, erasing the scowling lines from his grim features with a smooth fingertip. "Our babe is going to know a happy man for a pa—a man full of smiles, laughter, and praise for the Lord!"

Alton looked down at her. When he spoke, it was with a

lightness his heavy heart could not feel. "That sounds like a tall order, Sue, 'specially for a man who feels unfittin' and woeful inexperienced."

"It *is* a tall order," Sue Ellen responded seriously. "Any man can be a sire, Alton, but it takes a true man to be a pa—as you've been for my Jem and will be for our little one, too. Don't doubt yourself, Alton. After all, the Lord granted my prayers asking for a young 'un to bless our marriage. This is His plan for us—He'll see us through."

From that day forward Alton was a man with a fresh sense of purpose. It seemed as if every waking hour was spent in hard labor, but it was work that lifted his heart even when his body grew weary with exhaustion.

No effort seemed too great as he tended the crops, oversaw the livestock, and worked side by side with Jeremiah to provide the winter's supply of seasoned firewood needed to stoke the hearth and fire the cookstove.

When the work in the fields was done, Alton tended the yard so that it was a place of beauty. Sue Ellen took great comfort in her flowers, and when visitors came after the day's work, they admired them, too, with Sue Ellen swaddled beneath lap robes and shawls that shielded her condition from prying eyes.

As Indian summer's heat gave way to the cool rains of autumn, Alton savored content unlike any he had known. With work a way of life, he, like Sue Ellen, looked forward to the Lord's Day when they could enjoy the rest and fellowship with friends who dropped by to spend some leisure hours with the Wheelers.

While the menfolk enjoyed a game of horseshoes or arm wrestling, or discussed remedies for common livestock maladies, the women spent their afternoons exchanging recipes and news of the neighbors while busying their hands with mending or fancywork.

When Sue Ellen's condition grew obvious, Fanny remained with her when it wasn't fitting for Sue Ellen to socialize, assisting in stitching together the tiny baby garments stacking up in a neat pile in the chifforobe near the waiting cradle Alton had constructed.

"I'll be keepin' the needles flyin'," Fanny confided, shoving a thimbled fingertip against the needle as she darted it back and forth along the seam, almost as fast as the eye could see. "And," she added, looking up from her work with a knowing smile, "soon's I finish helpin' you sew for your babe, I'll be lendin' a hand to my Lizzie."

At the announcement, Sue Ellen regarded her friend in surprise. "Lizzie's going to have another wee one?"

"It's early yet," Fanny nodded, "but yes. The Lord willin', Thad will be seein' his second season when the new 'un arrives."

"I'm so happy for her," Sue Ellen murmured, "and frankly, for me, too. I hope our babies will grow up to be best of friends. Now I'll know my little one will have a ready playmate."

Fanny grinned. "Funny you should say that, Sue Wheeler. Your words echo the very ones that came from Lizzie's own mouth when she told me she was in the family way again, with her two months along already."

"How time flies," Sue Ellen said.

"Your time will be here before we know it," Fanny remarked, observing the rounded contours of her friend's middle. "If you're wantin', I'll be with you to midwife when your time comes."

Sue Ellen's needlework fell forgotten into her lap as she clasped her hands together in a gesture of gratitude. "Fanny, I'd like nothing better than to have you here. To be truthful,

I've worried that the doctor might not be able to come in time—especially if Salt Creek is flooded or icebound. It will certainly be a burden lifted from my mind to know that you're willing to help bring my babe into this world."

The older woman reached across and patted Sue Ellen's arm. "Consider it my promise given," she assured. "And know, too, that I consider it an honor to be present for your baby's birthin'." Fanny kicked back in the rocker and set the chair in motion.

"Just think," she finally spoke again, "might be that you'll have your baby by Christmas. Wouldn't it be a special blessin' to present the Lord with a new soul to love Him on the day markin' the Savior's birthday?"

Sue Ellen glanced up quickly. *How like Fanny to perceive the secret of my heart,* she thought. "I've been hoping for that. In fact, I've been turning it over in my mind. If I have my Christmas child and if it's a girl, I want to name her Mary Katharine—in honor of Christ's mother and Alton's mama. And, if the Lord should give me a son, I'd fancy calling him Joseph Alton—in remembrance of the devoted, loving man who was to the Lord Jesus what Alton's been to my Jeremiah."

Fanny halted her rocking to stare in awe. "Sue! That's right thoughtful—and a truly beautiful sentiment," she declared. "With a faithful, gentle heart like yours, surely the Lord will answer you and bless your hopes. The first of the New Year would be nice, of course, but I'll be prayin' right along with you that we get a Christmas babe. I'll ask Lizzie to mention it when she talks to the Lord, too."

Sue Ellen sighed. "I wouldn't mind the baby coming early so it will be over," she confided. "Some days it feels that I've been in this condition always." And she shifted in her chair for a position that would ease the aching in her back.

Fanny's brows folded into a frown. "I know how that is,"

41

she commiserated. "The waitin' seems to go on forever, doesn't it?"

Sue Ellen squinted to pick at a thread, then smoothed the seam and began stitching. "I probably sound ungrateful, wishing it was over and done, with a healthy babe in my arms early," she confessed. "And sometimes I get scared for even allowing myself to feel and think that way. Blessings have been piling up all around, Fanny, until sometimes I can't help but fear something's going to destroy such happiness."

"Bosh!" the older woman snorted emphatically.

But when Fanny turned away on the pretext of threading her needle, she was careful not to let Sue Ellen see, mirrored in her own face, the fears and concerns reflected in her young friend's weary green gaze.

For a few minutes they worked in silence. Then, to banish the disturbing quiet that had enveloped them, Fanny said comfortingly, "You're just sufferin' the worryin' natural to a woman in the motherly way, honey. Why, when a woman's ripe with child, I swear, she can find cause to wonder if the sun is goin' to come up in the east and settle down at night in the west!"

Sue Ellen smiled and laughed weakly. "I suppose you're right."

"I know I am!" Fanny said. "So hush your mouth, girl, and cast your silly fears and worries behind you. Don't even let yourself be thinkin' 'em!"

"I won't," Sue Ellen promised, but a shadow still remained that dulled the sparkle of her green eyes.

chapter
3

SOME DAYS it seemed that Sue Ellen's fears were compounded and magnified by almost everyone she saw and everything that happened. She contented herself that the unsettling emotions would pass, as Fanny had insisted, with the birth of her child.

October dragged by, and Sue Ellen ponderously journeyed through the wearying days. The bulk of her baby hampered every movement. She was powerless to position herself comfortably, and restful nights eluded her. Dark circles smudged beneath her eyes. Her cheeks grew thin, the fine bones prominent. Her once dewy blush of good health gave way to a sickly pallor.

"You'd better rest more," Alton ordered softly. "The doctor warned that it's a big task bringin' a new life into the world."

"I know, but I . . ." Sue Ellen's words faded away.

"Stay in—and stay warm!" Alton said. He snugged the comforter around her as she warmed herself by the fire. Reaching for a stocking in the woven basket, she threaded a needle and began to darn.

A moment later Sue Ellen leaned back in the rocker, the needle motionless. "I think I sit too much!" she protested.

"Truly, it might do me good to go outside and walk in the fresh air."

Hunkered beside the hearth, Alton studied her, reflecting on her words. "Mebbe you're right, sweetheart," he said gently. "We'll do some walkin' in the woods. The leaves are right pretty now—all blazin' with color."

"I'd like that," she said, setting aside her work before he could change his mind. "Could we go now?" She boosted herself from the rocker. "I'll just get a wrap—"

"All right," Alton agreed reluctantly. "But promise me you'll turn back the minute you start to tire."

The breeze was balmy, the afternoon kissed by the sun, as the two slowly walked the trails, savoring the pleasant moments spent planning and dreaming.

"Gettin' tired?" Alton asked, halting, when Sue Ellen paused to lean against a sycamore tree and placed her hand at the small of her back.

She drew in a deep breath and gave him a feeble, but bright, smile. "No, let's walk on a little ways. Please."

Seeing a rusty strand of barbed wire barring their passage ahead, Alton placed a booted foot on the sagging fence and bore down. Sue Ellen accepted his steadying grip as she held her skirts high and stepped over.

A few paces into the deeper woods, Alton halted, sniffing the air. "That's strange ... I smell smoke."

Sue Ellen lifted her head, detecting the acrid smell in her nostrils. "I do, too. It's been so dry—I hope it's not fire in the timber."

Alton shook his head. "It's not leaves and timberland ablaze, Sue. It's the scent of chimney smoke." He frowned. "We wouldn't be havin' new neighbors 'thout us knowin' 'bout it, would we?"

"I wouldn't think so." Sue Ellen's dark brows furrowed

with concern. "Why, the deserted Bannon farm is the only one I know of in these parts, and the house is little more than a lean-to. It's scarcely fit to serve as a dwelling. Besides, no one's said a word about new neighbors."

"Mebbe no one's said anythin'—because no one knew."

They walked on, but Sue Ellen could not dismiss the matter from her mind. "Seems odd that someone would move into the community without notice and without bothering to become acquainted with other folks—downright unfriendly, in fact."

In her musings Sue Ellen had failed to notice that Alton was steering her in the direction of their homestead. "After I get you back to the cabin, I'll do some investigatin'."

Sue Ellen halted in her tracks. "I could go with you."

But Alton shook his head, urging her on. "It's quite a ways to the Bannon property. I won't have you taxin' yourself. We'll walk again tomorrow, if it's fit weather."

"Yes, but—" Sue Ellen would not be denied.

"No buts. I'll drive you over to the Bannon property myself so you can go callin', if, indeed, we do have new neighbors," he promised, laughing. "I know how you womenfolk are, wantin' to lend a hand 'n' all."

No sooner had Alton returned Sue Ellen to the cabin than he struck out for the Bannon property. Within the hour he returned.

"We've new neighbors all right."

"Did you make their acquaintance?" Sue Ellen called from the hearth as Alton washed up in the basin in the kitchen.

Alton shook his head as if to clear it of the scene he had witnessed from his vantage point on the wooded hillside overlooking the tumble-down shanty. At the remembrance his jaw flexed and helpless loathing burned in his stomach for the craven coward of a man who would strike the pale, bony

45

woman—scarcely more than a girl—who was with child, farther along even than his Sue Ellen, until she bawled with hurt and humiliation.

"I said—did you make their acquaintance?" Sue Ellen repeated her question in a louder tone.

"No," Alton said. "Didn't want to intrude."

Sue Ellen laughed. "Oh, Alton! I'm sure they wouldn't have minded." She paused thoughtfully. "What were they like? Did you see any young'uns?"

"No young'uns, though the woman is with child. What are they like? Oh, hard to tell," Alton said softly, not wanting to pass judgment. "Just folks, I reckon."

How could he describe to Sue Ellen that poor wretch he had seen? From the looks of it, she was a woman of loose morals, maybe a saloon girl who had married unwisely. Further, why should he worry and upset his wife, who had enough concerns of her own without fussing and stewing over the lot of an unfortunate young woman subject to a niggardly man's cruel abuse?

"We should be neighborly, Alton, even if they haven't been," Sue Ellen said reproachfully.

"Maybe they druther be left alone—"

"Maybe they're just shy and waiting on us to introduce ourselves," she persisted. "How old do they appear to be? Have you any idea how long they've been in these parts?"

Sue Ellen waited expectantly, and Alton knew she would not cease with her questions until he had answered them to her satisfaction.

"How long? Well, do you recollect when Rusty, that Rhode Island Red hen Fanny gave us, got carried off by a raccoon or a fox? Or so we figgered—"

"Yes," Sue Ellen answered, frowning.

"Well, Rusty ended up in our new neighbors' stewpot. Her feathers were all over. I'd know that hen's colorin' anywhere!"

"Rusty *was* an unusual color," Sue Ellen admitted, digesting the news. Then a frown troubled her face, and with great effort she heaved herself from her chair. "Those poor people!" she cried, wringing her hands as she crossed to the window and peered out across the pasture in the direction of their pitiful hovel. "If only they'd come around to acquaint themselves with the neighbors, they'd have found us generous people, more than willing to share our bounty. Regardless of the past, Alton, *we're* going to do something!" Sue Ellen's ideas flowed. "We've potatoes in the cellar, preserves on the shelf, and we've some cured hams still hanging in the smokehouse, and us with shoats ready to butcher as soon as it's cold enough next month." Her voice rose with her mounting enthusiasm.

"Sue—"

"First thing tomorrow morning," she went on, "after I have bread fresh from the oven, we're going calling on the neighbors. If they stole—borrowed—our hen, we'll give them more besides. Like the Good Book says, if a man demands your coat, give him your cloak as well! You know how good the neighbors were to us—it's only fitting and fair that we pass on the favor."

"Whatever you say," Alton said, hoping, even as he knew better, that Sue Ellen would give up her crusade by morning.

But the next day found Sue Ellen bustling around long before sunup. Bread was rising in the pan when Alton came into the kitchen for breakfast. Before he could seat himself, Sue Ellen informed him that she'd have the fresh bread and vittles packed in the hamper and ready to go calling by midmorning.

"I'll have the team ready," Alton promised, sighing, his reluctance in the matter audible.

Sue Ellen gave him a stern stare. "I'm surprised at you, Alton Wheeler!" she scolded. "How can you be unwilling to help someone less fortunate when we've been so greatly blessed?"

After a long moment, there was contrition in Alton's voice when he spoke. "You're right, Sue," he said. "The Good Book does say that anything done for the least of the brethren is the same as doin' for the Lord Himself. Reckon there's room on the buckboard for a small jag of firewood," he mused as he threw on a heavy jacket to go outdoors. "I noticed they didn't have but a few twigs ricked up, and winter's wind is already breathin' across the land."

The sternness melted from Sue Ellen's face, replaced by a warm glow of admiration. "You're a good man, Alton Wheeler," she said, hugging him. As the baby shifted between them, Alton dropped an adoring kiss to her smooth forehead.

"It's only 'cause I've got me such a fine woman to set the example," he whispered.

En route to the pasture to call the team, Alton shuddered when he thought of the encounter that was about to take place between his Sue and the new neighbors. He prayed that the fight that had raged in their tangled, briar-choked yard, with the woman screaming curses that would have failed the lips of many a man after her bullying husband issued a bone-cracking slap to her face, had been forgotten and that Sue Ellen would discover apparent domestic harmony.

When Alton and Sue Ellen arrived a half-hour later, the Bannon farm seemed devoid of life, except for the thin stream of smoke curling from the crumbling chimney.

When he drew the team into the unkempt yard and pulled around to the rear of the shanty, Alton spotted the woman, bloated with child, humped over a rusty washtub. Soap bubbles clung to her reddened, chapped hands. Wearily, she rested her weight on the worn washboard, one leg of which was wired into place.

Dan nickered. The woman jerked around with a start, surprise registering in her vacant eyes before fear took root and replaced it.

"How do!" she hailed them in a shrill tone, brushing her matted, bleached hair from her face as she offered them an uncertain smile.

Alton called a greeting and turned to help Sue Ellen from the wagon. Quickly she walked over to the woman who was wiping her hands on her faded dress because she had no apron.

"Hello! I'm Sue Ellen Wheeler and this is my husband, Alton. We've come to welcome you to our community."

The girl stood, stupefied, and Sue Ellen chattered on, gradually winning the haggard young woman's confidence.

"My name's Maybelle," said the woman at last. "An' my man's Arnie . . . uh, Arnie . . . *Bannon*. Some kin o' Arnie's own this farm an' . . ." Her words trailed off and she cast a nervous glance toward the door of the shanty before clamping her lips against further idle speech.

"I know how difficult it is to set up housekeeping in a new place," Sue Ellen went on smoothly. "It seems you're always short of something you can't do without and forgot to buy. I've brought you a few things to help out."

"Oh, we're much obliged, ma'am!"

Alton felt almost ill when the woman's eyes skipped hungrily to the back of the buckboard where the hamper rested. She seemed to be trembling with eagerness to examine its contents.

"I'd invite y'all into the cabin . . . b—but my man . . . he's sick . . . dreadful sick. An' when he don't feel good, he's—"

"We don't want to intrude," Sue Ellen interrupted her halting speech. "Alton can carry the hamper to the doorstoop. And you could unpack the things there and carry them into the cabin."

"That's a right fine idea!" she agreed cheerfully.

She trailed Alton and Sue Ellen to the wagon, followed them to the doorstoop, then with plucky strength, spirited the hamper inside the rickety dwelling and a moment later returned with it, emptied of its treasures.

"My, but you must be a fine cook, Miz Wheeler," said the woman. "The food smells so tasty. Arnie and I are grateful an' give you our thanks 'til you're better rewarded."

"Please call me Sue Ellen."

"If you'll call me Maybelle," she countered, beaming broadly.

"Well then . . . Maybelle," Sue Ellen said in a light voice, "we can visit a bit while Alton unloads the wood. Then we'll leave so you can be about your business and tend to your husband's needs."

"I'll 'preciate the company."

She knelt again on the moist ground in front of the washtub, sopping her muddy skirt, and plunged her hands into the chilly water. She looked up at Sue Ellen, gave her a wry, sisterly smile, and mopped a stray lock of hair away from her forehead with a dripping hand.

"I couldn't help noticin' that you're cursed to carry a man's seed, too," Maybelle sighed.

Sue Ellen blanched, recoiling at the words. She was about to correct her, making clear that bearing a babe wasn't a curse but a blessing. But she stemmed the words when she realized that the girl's bitter plight was far different from her own.

50

Poor Maybelle's baby was as unwanted as her own child was desired.

"I'd noticed, too," Sue Ellen said. "When will your babe come, Maybelle?"

The slattern shrugged. "This week—next. Whenever it's ready, I reckon."

"Have you seen a doctor?"

Maybelle gave a harsh chortle. "Arnie don't have much use for a sawbones. Besides, doctorin' costs money. That's something there ain't much of. What there is . . . Arnie keeps to himself . . . or gambles away."

"What will you do when your time comes, Maybelle?" Sue Ellen murmured worriedly.

The girl gave her a bovine stare and another helpless shrug of her bony shoulders.

"Don't rightly know, Miz Wheeler . . . Sue Ellen . . . as this ain't never happened to me before. But I reckon I'll get through it some way or t'other. Women always has . . . women always will."

"Yes, that's true," Sue Ellen mused, preoccupied. "But you really should have someone to help you . . . especially with your first." The gravity of the situation emboldened Sue Ellen to make an offer. "Would your husband . . . mind . . . if I were to come, be your midwife, when it's time?"

Again Maybelle shrugged and slung a garment to the brown grass, shook water from her hands, and vigorously squeezed and twisted the soggy item. "Dunno. Arnie's as changeable as the wind. One minute he's full o' laughter and good times . . . and the next . . . well. . . . Maybe he'd mind . . . maybe he wouldn't."

Scarcely had the two women begun discussing Arnie than he appeared in the doorway of the shanty. A dark scowl, so fearsome that it chilled Sue Ellen to the marrow of her bones,

51

shrouded his features. Maybelle stared at the man, with stark fear in her haunted eyes.

"Hello, Mister Bannon!" Sue Ellen called out warmly, covering the awkward moment. "We're your new neighbors. We live up the road a piece." She crossed to Arnie and extended her hand as if she believed him a gentleman, well-born, and she expected no less courtesy from him.

The fierce glare left Arnie's narrow face. Alton watched with amused disgust as the man adopted a different pose, one he seemed to believe would appeal to the genteel woman who'd come to welcome them to the community.

"My husband is unloading a bit of firewood," Sue Ellen gestured in Alton's direction. "He'll be making your acquaintance when he's through. He reckoned that you could use some wood—moving in so late in the year—with winter just around the corner."

"Many thanks. We're in debt to you," Arnie Bannon said smoothly, and gave Sue Ellen a practiced grin that curved his lips but did not travel to his hard, dark eyes.

"Not at all," Sue Ellen corrected. "Repay the debt, if you would, by passing the favor on to another. That's what Fanny Preston told me when I was new to this community." Sue Ellen drew a careful breath. "And, speaking of Fanchon Preston—Fanny is probably the best midwife in these parts. Maybelle's so new to Salt Creek community that I'm wagering she probably hasn't had time to find a doctor or seek a woman to help her when her time draws nigh. But since we're your closest neighbors, I'd consider it an honor if you'd call on me, Mister Bannon."

Sue Ellen smiled at Arnie, but her eyes darted to Maybelle, feeling almost ill when she confronted the intensity of the hope in the girl's faded blue eyes.

"If it strikes your fancy." He shrugged but didn't object.

"I'll be here," Sue Ellen promised, relieved. "When Maybelle's time comes, you just call on us. I'll keep a bag packed in readiness, so I can be here on a moment's notice."

"Much obliged, ma'am," Arnie said, and gave her a quick nod before he passed by to help Alton stack the firewood.

Maybelle halted her scrubbing to stare up with such wondrous appreciation that it brought tears prickling to Sue Ellen's eyes.

"Thank you, ma'am," Maybelle whispered tremulously. "I've been so scared about the babe comin' . . . afeared that Arnie'd be off or layin' in bed dead drunk. You've set my mind to ease. You can't know what it means to me."

Sue Ellen touched Maybelle's shoulder tenderly. "Yes, I can," she said. "I know the relief I felt when Fanny promised to be there for me. The Lord is always faithful to tend to our needs."

Maybelle leaned back on her haunches. With a damp hand she smoothed back her hair, momentarily subduing the brassy curls.

"Maybe for you," Maybelle whispered, returning to her scrubbing as if unable to meet Sue Ellen's serene eyes a moment longer, "but not for someone like . . . me."

"Of course for you, too!" Sue Ellen assured. "I'm here now, aren't I? And I will be here when your time comes just as soon as Arnie brings your message."

"About Arnie . . . ," Maybelle began reluctantly, "he has a habit of runnin' off. For days at a time. It worries me to death. But sometimes him runnin' off is a durn sight better than having him at home, ragin' an' complainin' an' findin' fault with every breath I draw—"

"Don't you worry, Maybelle," Sue Ellen whispered. "Alton and I have started taking long walks so I can get some fresh air. I'll come by every day to check on you, and on the days when the weather is bad, I'll ask my boy to drop by—"

"Please, no!" Maybelle cried, her eyes wide with horror as she stared up at Sue Ellen. "Don't send no young man around here! When Arnie gets jealous . . . and full of his accusations . . . he's a beast. No doubt your boy's a nice fellow an' all, but if he started droppin' by, Arnie'd think the worst."

"Oh, dear," Sue Ellen murmured. "Perhaps you can leave a sign."

She slipped her lace handkerchief from her cuff and gave it to Maybelle. After casting a furtive glance in Arnie's direction, the woman stuffed the now-damp scrap of cloth down the bosom of her dress.

"When your time comes, hang the hanky on the clothesline, Maybelle. I'll have Jem slip through the woods and look for it every evening right before sundown. Don't worry. He'll keep out of sight."

Tears glimmered in Maybelle's eyes. She stared at Sue Ellen a long, grateful moment.

"This Lord o' yours . . . He sure provides you with quick answers . . . don't He?"

Sue Ellen nodded. "The Lord helps those who have the wisdom to seek His guidance. Trust Him, Maybelle. He'll take care of you and your babe, as well."

"I'll try, ma'am," Maybelle promised. "But how do you go about talkin' to somebody you can't see?"

"Sue! Are you ready to go?" Alton called.

"I'll be right there," Sue Ellen called back, giving Maybelle's shoulder a reassuring squeeze. "We'll talk later," she said in a low tone. "Now that we're friends, there will be other times."

Maybelle arose from her knees, dripping water as she walked to the wagon with Sue Ellen. Her wet shoes damply sucked against the hard ground.

"I sure hate to see you go, Sue Ellen."

"I'll be back to see you very soon, don't worry."

"Tomorrow?" Maybelle ventured hopefully.

"If the weather's fit, you can count on it."

"Good," Maybelle whispered. "Arnie's runnin' low on liquor. I 'spect he'll be goin' in search of more. God knows when he'll be back." She studied the ground before her. "Sometimes I 'low as how I'd be better off if he never returned. Yet . . . I love 'im. Arnie don't do nothin' to deserve my love," Maybelle said sadly, "but I care about 'im even so. I guess that sounds plumb stupid to you, Sue Ellen."

"I understand perfectly," Sue Ellen nodded, "because that's the kind of love the Lord has for us. He loves us even when we're bad, loves us when we're good, loves us so much that His Son, Jesus Christ, died for us."

Maybelle shook her head. "I love Arnie. Don't know that I love the poor blighter enough to die for 'im, though." She shrugged helplessly. "But, then, I reckon a person wouldn't know about that 'til the time came to do it."

"Sue!" Alton reminded.

Impulsively Sue Ellen gave Maybelle a hug. "I'll be back tomorrow."

"I'll be waitin'," Maybelle admitted. "And I'm hopin' that Arnie will be away for a while . . . so's we can talk private . . . an' you can tell me about this Lord o' yours." She halted, shaking her head in confusion. "Don't rightly understand it, Sue Ellen, but it makes me feel kind of good somehow, hearin' you talk about God that way . . . like He's a good friend or somethin'."

Sue Ellen smiled, turning to take Alton's hand and climbing awkwardly into the wagon.

He nodded to the Bannons and clucked to the team, the wheels of the wagon moving slowly over the rutted road. Lost in their own thoughts, there was no conversation for the first few minutes.

"Now you've met the new neighbors," Alton stated flatly after turning the team onto the trail leading home.

"I liked Maybelle," Sue Ellen said. "Beneath that hard, coarse surface, there is a very pleasant young woman."

"And behind Arnie Bannon's wide smile—" The ugly words failed Alton as he refused to give verbal witness to the menacing evils that had been revealed despite Arnie's attempt to hide them.

"He's not a nice man . . . not nice at all," Sue Ellen agreed. "But I'm going back to visit with Maybelle anyway! Arnie Bannon can't scare me away!"

Alton scratched his black hair and adjusted his felt hat. "I doubt he'd try, sweetheart. You had Arnie eatin' out o' your hand. I don't rightly know how you managed it with such a braggarty, salty-tongued devil—"

"With the Lord's help and the wisdom of His Word, quite easily," Sue Ellen said lightly. "A kind word turns away wrath every time."

chapter
4

WHEN DAWN heralded a fresh morning Sue Ellen began her day. Trying not to appear rushed so Alton wouldn't complain, she whipped together biscuits and sausage gravy.

After giving the cabin a lick and a promise, Sue Ellen packed leftover biscuits and a small bowl of gravy into a reed basket. Leaving a note on the table to alert Alton to her whereabouts, she set out on her leisurely walk to the Bannon shanty.

Even though she took her time, Sue Ellen was puffing with each breath, and the baby kicked against her rib cage in protest to the unaccustomed activity.

"You came!" Maybelle cried, delighted when Sue Ellen appeared at her door. "Arnie's gone away!" she added cheerfully. "Come in! I've got water heatin' for tea. 'Tain't much, though, just some leaves, roots, and herbs I gathered. I remembered my mama brewin' it when I was a child. Hope it tastes pleasin'." Maybelle frowned. "The only trouble is I can't recollect exactly what leaves Mama used. She died when I was a child, leavin' me an' my older sister Dorcas alone with Pappy." She gave a characteristic shrug and grinned. "But he run off in no time. . . . Reckon he was a lot like my Arnie."

Maybelle led Sue Ellen into the grime-encrusted dwelling.

Even her obvious attacks with mop and broom hadn't successfully routed the filth, so she had apparently surrendered.

"They say the fruit don't fall far from the tree," Maybelle smiled sheepishly, noticing Sue Ellen's look of distaste. "For my part, I reckon it's true. My plight's no better'n my mama's was."

"You've a sister named Dorcas?" Sue Ellen inquired politely.

"Last I knew I did. But there's no guarantee she's still around. Ain't seen Dorcas in years. We both went to work in a saloon in Chicago not long after Pappy skeedaddled."

"I see," Sue Ellen said stiffly.

Maybelle turned her back to Sue Ellen. "I figgered you had sized me up for what I am . . . was." Shame tinged her soft tone. "A woman alone . . . there ain't many ways to survive. I done what I had to," she added defensively.

"The Lord doesn't care about the woman you've been— only the one you are—and the one you want to be, Maybelle," Sue Ellen said gently. "We've all made mistakes. In fact, it's because of those mistakes that God sent His Son as a tiny babe, to abide with us, redeem us from all our wrongdoing, and show us a better way to live."

"My Granny, she used to talk like that," Maybelle recalled as she poured the weak brew into chipped cups. "I was just a wee mite, so I scarcely recollect anything a'tall. But hearin' you talk kind of makes me miss those days when I was a young'un at her knee, listenin' to stories of miracles."

"Do you have a Bible, Maybelle?" Sue Ellen asked. "I have a spare Testament. It's yours if you'd like it."

Maybelle stared at her roughened hands with their short, broken nails. "Would love to have it, a gift from you, Sue Ellen. I'd cherish it for that reason alone. But fat lot of good

58

it'd do me—ownin' a pretty book—bein' as I can't read. And if I had call to write my name, I'd have to do it with a sign."

"You never had a chance to learn writing or ciphering?" Sue Ellen murmured.

"No, but even if I could, Arnie'd try to spoil it for me somehow. He'd never 'low such a fine thing in the house, if he thought it pleasured me."

"Just try to live like the Lord would want, Maybelle," Sue Ellen suggested. "And perhaps your example will change Arnie and help him become the kind of man you'd like him to be. My Alton hasn't always been a godly man, either."

As the minutes passed and they sipped their tea companionably, Sue Ellen told the story of her tumultuous love for Alton and his wayward path that had at last led to a strong commitment to Christ.

"The Good Book says that a virtuous woman is a man's greatest treasure and that a woman can help her spouse find the Lord through her own faith and godly conduct."

"Mebbe so, but I wouldn't bet on it," Maybelle said with a trace of despair. "'Sides, I ain't on such good terms with the Good Lord myself. Don't know Him like you do, Sue Ellen."

"Then I'll be praying that you'll find Him as your own Savior first. Just as I'll be praying that this birth will be an easy one. The coming of the babe may work to change Arnie, too," Sue Ellen offered encouragement. "No doubt many a man has reformed his ways with the coming of a child."

"That might happen for some," Maybelle sighed, "but I'm not holdin' out much hope. Poor little mite." She rubbed her swollen belly. "Can't help feelin' bad about bringin' this'un into the world. My lot's miserable enough but what chance does this babe have with an ignorant saloon-girl for a mama and an ornery, bullyin' drunk for a pa?"

Sue Ellen was momentarily without words. "The Lord gave

your babe life, Maybelle, and it's not up to us to question His wisdom. Rejoice in the coming of your infant, Maybelle. There is a reason for all this, whether we understand it or not."

"I *am* looking forward to the babe," Maybelle admitted. "Arnie don't love me . . . but maybe this child will . . . and then I'll have *somebody* to care about me."

"Of course your child will love you!" Sue Ellen exclaimed. "But you're wrong about not being loved. *God* loves you and *I* love you! I felt Christian love for you even before we met. Now my love for you is growing stronger as I get to know you better."

"You're real sweet to say such nice things, Sue Ellen," Maybelle said, blinking rapidly. "If nothing else good ever happens in my life, I'll consider myself blessed that our paths crossed."

On the way home Sue Ellen prayed for her unhappy, burdened young friend. After giving orders for Maybelle to rest while Arnie was away, Sue Ellen could only hope that she was taking her advice to heart. Poor Maybelle looked so haggard already that Sue Ellen feared for the trials she would face in delivering the large baby from her exhausted body.

Three days later, feeling the strain of her own advanced pregnancy, Sue Ellen's entire being throbbed in weary protest as she prepared the evening meal.

The sun was slanting low in the west and Sue Ellen had just placed plates and cutlery on the table when Jem rushed into the cabin.

"Your hanky's on the Bannons' line!" he cried, gasping for breath, his thin shoulders heaving. "There was no sign of light in the house but—"

Sue Ellen closed her eyes momentarily and prayed for

strength. "Please ask Alton to hitch the team, Jem," Sue Ellen said quietly. "Maybelle's in need."

Ignoring her own fatigue, Sue Ellen stoically packed a hamper with the items she would need.

Alton, too, was grim when he came in with news that the team was hitched. "I put in extra lanterns in case they're short on coal oil."

"Thank you, Alton. That was thoughtful of you," Sue Ellen smiled wearily. "I have a stack of fresh linens, and the hamper's packed with supplies." Alton picked up the load. Sue Ellen wrapped her cloak around her, shivering as she followed him to the wagon. "After you take me to Maybelle's—if you don't mind—would you go to Fanny's and see if she's free to come help me?"

"That was my plan," Alton admitted.

The Bannon shanty was dark when they arrived. Sue Ellen rapped on the door, but there was no answer. A tortured groan from within prompted them to enter without invitation. Alton's lantern arced around the room, chasing shadows on the walls, as they progressed to the tiny nook off the main room.

The ashes in the grate were cold. Maybelle, dazed with pain, lay swaddled in grimy quilts.

"I'll light a fire, put on a kettle of water, and do what needs doin' for your safety before I leave for Fanny's," Alton assured her, "though I wish we'd thought to send Jem with the message. 'Twould be best if I didn't have to leave you."

Sue Ellen set right to work to make Maybelle more comfortable, while Alton quickly kindled a fire, lit the lamps, fetched water from the cistern, and set it over the fire. Then, at Sue Ellen's request, he helped her place fresh bedding beneath the young woman's tormented form.

"I'll go now, if you're sure there ain't nuthin' else I can do here," Alton said.

"Godspeed!" Sue Ellen whispered, smoothing the lank strands of Maybelle's sweat-matted hair away from her face.

After Alton had left, Sue Ellen knotted a sheet and closed Maybelle's fingers around it, encouraging her to pull against the pains, scream if she wanted but rest assured that Sue Ellen would not leave her until the task was completed and the baby safely born.

The minutes dragged out like hours. Helplessly Sue Ellen listened to Maybelle's screams and moans. At times the woman resorted to loud curses, only to gasp out apologies to Sue Ellen for subjecting her to such a display.

Maybelle's body grew rigid with terror. She fought the spasms that rippled through her small frame, then strained to produce the child that awaited the moment of birth. Sue Ellen sponged her brow and whispered words of consolation, all the while listening, praying to be rewarded by the sound of the soft clip-clop of horses' hooves, signaling Alton's return. But there was no sound outside the cabin—only the tortured moans of the laboring woman.

Feeling a mounting sensation of helplessness, and in the face of the vile expletives issuing from Maybelle, Sue Ellen began to pray aloud. It was a long moment before she realized that the shrieks had ceased. Maybelle lay still, panting between the contractions that contorted her body. Her eyes, once glazed with terror and pain, now focused on Sue Ellen.

The prayer on Sue Ellen's lips trailed away—

"I'm sorry," Maybelle whimpered. "I plumb forgot what you told me, Sue . . . that the Lord would see me through this . . . if I'd just remember to trust in Him to take care of me."

Sue Ellen gave a tired smile. "I'm no better, darlin'," she comforted the frightened girl. "It almost slipped my mind, too. But we can be sure He won't forsake us when we need Him most."

Again the birth pangs gripped Maybelle, and she uttered a faint moan.

"Push . . . and pray!" Sue Ellen coaxed.

She took Maybelle's hand, replacing the knotted rag with her comforting grip. "Good . . . good. You're doing just fine," Sue Ellen whispered, squeezing Maybelle's hand. "Your fine young'un will be here in no time."

But it wasn't.

Shortly afterward Alton, followed by Fanny Preston, entered the poor shanty. Sue Ellen had never been so glad to see anyone in her life!

"Get yourself home, girl!" ordered Fanny. "You're in no condition to help anyone—"

But Sue Ellen was adamant. "Fanchon Preston, I know you're far more competent than I, but Maybelle Bannon is my friend. I gave her my word that I'd be with her for her babe's birthing, and remain here I will!"

Fanny relented. "Then be a good girl. Stay out of my way—an' off your feet—or I'll be havin' to move poor Maybelle over to make room for you!"

Seating herself on the lone chair in the house—a rickety, high-backed, mule-eared piece of furniture that gave support if not comfort—Sue Ellen passed the long night.

While Maybelle labored with Fanny's expert assistance and Sue Ellen slept fitfully, Alton nurtured the fire, keeping the howling wind at bay as best he could. But the determined gusts found entrance through the cracks in the poorly fitted planks and whistled down the chimney, causing Sue Ellen to shiver beneath her shawl. Concerned that she should take a chill, Alton kept close watch, feeding the blaze with the logs he had brought as a welcoming gift.

More than once he noticed small puffs of smoke escaping into the room from the chinks in the crude chimney. Such a sign bode ill indeed, he thought with alarm. A new mother and her babe would not fare well through the winter months without some way to capture the heat. And that scoundrel, Bannon, was not likely to stir himself to look out for his little family when the coldest weather set in. *I'll fill those cracks myself,* he vowed. *And re-chink the chimney, too. On the first fair day—*

Just then he heard an infant's cry. With the breaking of dawn Maybelle had at last given up her burden to the world.

"'Tis a fine son ye have!" Fanny announced. Holding the red, wrinkled manchild upside down, she delivered a smart smack to his tiny rump.

"He's beautiful, Maybelle," Sue Ellen assured her, rousing from her place beside the hearth to inspect the wee one. "A truly fine boy."

"And a blessing, that," Maybelle murmured in a bitter whisper. "At least the Lord granted me my hope that 'twould not be a poor girlchild to grow up and suffer a man's curse and know the misery of love—"

At these words, Fanny cast a troubled glance in Sue Ellen's direction. Responding to Maybelle's beckoning finger, Sue Ellen approached the bedside and bent low to hear her whispered words before the exhausted new mother drifted off into a deep sleep.

In the crude kitchen, Fanny bathed the newborn child and wrapped him in the clean linens Sue Ellen had provided.

"She's had a hard and bitter life," Sue Ellen explained in excuse for Maybelle's remarks.

Fanny sighed and placed a loving kiss on the sobbing babe's wrinkled face. "And it's likely to remain harsh and cruel for her . . . and the boy . . . God love an' keep 'em."

64

"Short of the Lord's own miracle, I'm afraid you're right," Sue Ellen sighed.

"And *I'm* afraid," Fanny said, changing the subject, "that if you don't get home and into bed, you're going to have a harsh time of it yourself. Now home with you . . . and don't let me hear nary a word of protest!"

Sue Ellen smiled. "Not one word of protest, Fanny, but a great many of thanks."

"And speaking of givin' thanks," Fanny said, "Will caught a wild gobbler in a snare, praise God! And he's got that feisty tom cooped up with all the corn that turkey can swallow. We're countin' on you folks breakin' bread . . . and carvin' turkey . . . with us on Thanksgivin' Day."

"We'll look forward to that," Sue Ellen readily accepted. "But I want to provide something—candied sweet potatoes and noodles in butter, perhaps? And maybe a pumpkin pie?"

Fanny shook her head. "You'll provide nothin' but hearty appetites!" she insisted. "Lizzie is already bakin' tarts and fancies, storin' them in her pantry. I'll take care of everything else."

"Speaking of Lizzie, how is she?" Sue Ellen asked, and instantly regretted her question when she saw the shadow of concern that crossed Fanchon's usually jovial features.

"She's feelin' none too pert," Fanny admitted. "She's sick the better part of most ever' day. We're prayin' that the sickness will pass quickly."

"I'll be praying for that, too."

"You skeedaddle home now, girl," Fanny reminded, "or we'll be prayin' over *you*."

Sue Ellen was almost asleep by the time Alton had made the wagon trip home, carried her to their room, and tucked her into bed.

Although Sue Ellen stoutly maintained that she was all

right, she knew that Alton's and Fanny's worries were not unfounded. The care rendered to Maybelle Bannon had extracted a toll on her meager strength.

The week passed, and she greeted Thanksgiving morn with relief that it heralded a day of celebration, relaxation, and fellowship with their friends instead of a day filled with tedious tasks.

Sue Ellen dressed with care before the journey to the Preston farm for the noon feast, and she and Alton entered the house, expecting to find Lizzie and Harmon Childers there ahead of them. Instead of the bustling activity that characterized Fanny's place, however, there was an ominous silence in the house.

Fanny was packing a hamper, her plump hands flying, as her tongue kept pace with orders delivered to a patient, waiting Will.

"What's wrong?" Sue Ellen cried. Her heart seemed to shrink and grow cold in her chest.

"It's Lizzie," Fanny said, continuing her packing. "She's down in bed this week. I didn't want to trouble you with the news, or carry upsetting thoughts to a woman in the motherly way, but . . . well, Lizzie lost her little 'un."

Sue Ellen's heart missed a beat, then resumed its steady thumping, stirred to life by her babe's sudden movement beneath her ribs. "Oh, Fanny, no!"

"It's the Lord's will," she spoke with confidence. "'The Lord giveth and the Lord taketh away.' There will be other babes."

"Of course there will," Sue Ellen echoed. "Poor Lizzie. She must be wild with grief."

"She's takin' it right hard," Fanny admitted. "Harm wanted her to come and be with us today and give thanks for the blessin's the Lord has showered on her. But she's wounded

66

with her loss and not capable of thinkin' in terms of blessin's, only what's been lost to her."

"It will pass," Sue Ellen said.

"'Course it will," Fanny agreed. "After all, many a time the Good Book says: 'And it came to pass,' never that it came to stay!"

The meal was delicious, but the celebration was subdued. By late afternoon Sue Ellen was growing visibly weary and, since Fanny and Will were to visit Lizzie later that evening, Alton suggested that they return to their farm earlier than planned.

"Except for poor Lizzie and Harm's sad news, it's been a wonderful day," Sue Ellen said to Alton on the way home. "But I wonder if you'd be so kind as to grant me one thing more? I'd like to see Maybelle Bannon. Could we, Alton?" she begged. "I haven't seen her but once since her child was born. I'd like to assure myself that she and the babe are all right."

"We can go right now if you'd like," Alton agreed. "I've been worryin' 'bout her myself. But with Bannon bein' the jealous kind, I thought it best not to inquire."

Jem hopped from the back of the buckboard and loped up the lane to begin his evening chores when Sue Ellen and Alton continued on toward the Bannon property.

"Oh, Lord—no!" Alton groaned as they topped a rise and were greeted by a cloud of black smoke drifting toward them.

Sue Ellen sniffed the air. This was not the pleasant tang of burning leaves, nor the homey scent of firewood sputtering in the grate. This was trouble!

Clutching the wagon seat for support, Sue Ellen hung on as Alton urged Doc and Dan on and the horses crashed down the hollows, jerking the bucking wagon behind.

Thick black smoke hung in the treetops, obscuring their

view. When they crested the last rise and the Bannon shanty came into sight, Sue Ellen screamed.

The lean-to was consumed in flames that shot from the windows and licked at the shake shingles, devouring the wood, until a portion of the roof that had been eaten away fell to the ground before their eyes.

Alton leaped from the wagon, glancing to the right and left for any sign of life. The place was a blazing inferno, and Doc and Dan reared in alarm as the acrid smoke spawned by the fire stung their nostrils.

At the sound of shrieks coming from behind the cabin, Sue Ellen jumped from the wagon, clutching her ribs as she landed with jarring impact. Hearing another anguished cry, she stumbled across the frozen turf, calling her friend's name.

"Maybelle!" Sue Ellen sobbed.

Alton reached her first.

Her face blank, she had been racing in dizzying circles, searching for a safe plot of ground on which to lay her child. But each time Maybelle stooped to put the babe down, she snatched him up again as sparks ignited the dead, brown grass nearby.

Leading the distraught woman to Sue Ellen's side, Alton set about to stamp out as many of the small brushfires as possible, realizing soon enough that it was a losing battle.

"Maybelle!" Sue Ellen drew her into the fringes of the yard.

"My baby! Keep my baby, Sue! I've got to go to Arnie! He's inside . . . layin' acrost the bed . . . dead drunk! I couldn't get him and the young'un both. Take my babe so's I can fetch Arnie from the fire—"

Sue Ellen caught the child an instant before Maybelle would have dropped him in her haste.

Maybelle whirled and streaked away.

SEASONS OF THE HEART

"Alton! Stop her!" Sue Ellen called. "She's going back to the shanty!"

"Maybelle!" Alton bellowed. "Stop—you cain't go in there! It ain't no use, he's not alive, woman! Stop!"

"Arnie needs me!" Maybelle cried and continued her desperate race. "Ain't no one in the world loves nor cares 'bout him but me. He needs me and I can't fail him—"

Alton sprinted ahead.

He could hardly breathe for the hot air that scorched his lungs and seared his face. Sparks sputtered in Maybelle's face, flaring like tinder in her bleached hair. She batted her arms wildly.

Squinting against the heat, Alton thundered after her, struggling to gain his footing. He reached out and was rewarded only by contact with the threadbare cotton gown that unfurled behind her as she ran. Knotting his fingers into the fabric, he held on tenaciously, sure that he had solid purchase with which to jerk the crazed woman back to safety.

But a moment later he was sprawled lengthwise on the cold, unyielding ground, mocked by the sound of ripping fabric. Unbelieving, he stared down at the pitiful scrap he still grasped in his hand. Maybelle was still weaving a staggering path to the door of the shanty.

"No!" Alton clawed to his feet, but he reeled backward from the force of the heat as the woman became a dark silhouette against the fire's glare.

With Maybelle's primal scream came Sue Ellen's hysterical shrieks. Alton stumbled to her side, shielding her from the flying sparks and the sight of the collapsing roof, burying the two inside a fiery coffin.

"It's over . . . ," Alton said. "Shhh, darlin', it's all over," he crooned, rocking Sue Ellen and the babe she held in her arms.

"Maybelle loved him," she said, choking on her tears. "She

69

loved Arnie—so much that she could die for him. And, Alton!" she cried, remembering Maybelle's whispered words on the day of her son's birth. "She said she knew the Lord had brought her through because He loved her, and that she felt like a newborn babe herself! Seems I can let her go so much easier—knowing she's with the Lord now."

Tears streamed down their faces as they stood, numbed, hunching against the bitter cold, the better to protect Maybelle's child between them.

With a harsh crack and hissing clatter, the brittle chimney gave way, raining sparks and flames and pronouncing a bizarre kind of benediction on Maybelle and Arnie.

"Poor babe—scarce born—'n' already an orphan."

"Perhaps an orphan, without a mama and a pa, but upon my word, never a child without love. I'll see to that!" Sue Ellen vowed.

"As will Fanny . . . 'n' Lizzie," Alton added.

Lizzie!

Alton considered the things that Fanny had said about Lizzie's grief in her loss. He looked at Sue Ellen, who sobbed quietly as he carefully guided the great Clydesdales down the familiar trail. Sue Ellen was weak, so frail she could hardly nurture the child beneath her heart, let alone the husky babe nestled on her lap.

"Perhaps Lizzie can keep the little'un for a while, Sue. When the word is out, some kin may come to claim the boy."

Sue Ellen turned her face away. "Well, I'll not be prevented from praying that no living relatives can be found so Lizzie and Harmon can raise this child as their own and guide him in the ways of the Lord."

Alton patted Sue Ellen's hand but kept his own counsel about the truth he'd discovered on that first day after witnessing the vicious fight between their new neighbors.

He'd let Sue Ellen believe Maybelle's story, and he would not tarnish her memory. He hoped his Sue would never have to know that Maybelle and Arnie were not man and wife and that their name was not even Bannon but was cleverly and carefully adopted to allay the suspicions of neighbors who might otherwise question their presence on the Bannon property.

With so little information about the pair, it was unlikely that there were relatives who would be wanting the little fellow anyway. The Lord would prevail.

"I'll be prayin' that, too," Alton promised. "An' hopin' that Lizzie and this lil' feller will discover a treasure of rich blessin's 'n' love."

chapter
5

FANNY PRESTON kept the orphaned babe overnight so Sue Ellen could recover her strength after her horrible ordeal. By the next evening Lizzie had claimed the tiny infant. When the authorities had no luck locating living relatives of the newborn child, Lizzie and Harm were allowed to consider the babe their own.

"We're callin' him 'Maylon'," Lizzie explained to Sue Ellen. "It's from the Bible . . . and because his mother's name was Maybelle."

Sue Ellen smiled. "How nice, Lizzie. I'm sure Maybelle would approve of that. And of you as his folks. My first thought was to keep Maybelle's baby and raise it as my own. But I've been so tired lately," she admitted with a sigh. "I really don't believe the Lord had it in mind for me. . . . Some days I wonder how I'll raise this one." She rested her hand on her abdomen.

Lizzie frowned. Younger than Sue Ellen by a good ten years, she had always admired the plucky woman, and she knew Sue Ellen Stone Wheeler had never been one to complain. She'd uttered not a word after helping to deliver Maybelle's babe, or after the shock of seeing the Bannon shanty burn to the ground with the two of them trapped

73

inside, or even, right lately, when Alton and Jeremiah had butchered two lardy shoats. Although Alton helped as best he could, and Fanny came to pitch in, there were many things that remained women's work, and Lizzie knew that as long as Sue Ellen could stand on her feet, she would do what was expected of her.

There was always so much to be done at hog-butchering time—salting and packing the meat for curing, frying the meat to be packed in heavy stone jars and sealed with boiling lard before being placed in the cellar. Even when others warned that Sue might suffer later if she didn't get her rest, she toiled on, forcing a smile in the face of their concern.

Lizzie gave Sue Ellen a loving hug. "Well, you'll do just fine!" Lizzie encouraged. "When Thad was born, I thought the time of confinement would *never* end. It seemed to drag out even worse when the time hovered near. It's natural to get weary, Sue, although you do look right peaked. You really should get more rest."

"You sound like Alton," Sue Ellen sighed. "I'll be glad when it's over. As near as I can figure, this babe should come with the New Year. But something in my heart tells me we won't wait that long."

"Maybe our prayers are bein' heard and you *will* have a Christmas child!"

"I'm praying so . . . if it's the will of the Lord," Sue Ellen said softly.

Christmas Eve day dawned bright, clear, and stingingly cold.

With the holiday on the morrow, Sue Ellen readied the family to attend worship services before returning for a traditional feast, and perhaps a visit with Fanny and Will's family later in the day.

Time flew by, but Sue Ellen's work lagged as she bit her lip to combat a nagging pain low in her back. There was so much yet to be done. Maybe, when her chores were done, she could sit a spell. She increased her tempo, ignoring the ache.

Chocolate fudge bubbled on the stove. When it had cooled sufficiently, Sue Ellen gratefully seated herself to whip the sticky syrup to a fluffy consistency. While she welcomed this brief reprieve, the brisk movement of her arm seemed to annoy the baby.

Still she worked, making the delectable holiday treats that Jem had come to expect each Christmas—and now Alton. Before she cleaned the kitchen, Sue Ellen had made caramels, popcorn balls, and even penuche and had arranged them, along with the squares of fudge, on a huge ironstone platter. Taking one last look around, she folded her apron and retired to her room, raising the lid of the trunk to make certain the small gifts for Jem and Alton were safely in place.

By nightfall Sue Ellen's bulging body shuddered with darting pangs of discomfort. She was so weary she could barely stand upright and sought a dram of comfort by hunching forward, almost protectively, over her precious burden. The supper hour found her with scarcely enough strength to lift her fork and with an appetite for nothing but sleep.

Tenderly Alton tucked Sue Ellen into bed, snugged the thick quilt beneath her chin, and smoothed her hair away from her cheek. She was asleep almost before he parted the curtain to exit the small room.

During the night, snow began to fall. Brutal gusts of wind howled around the corners of the cabin, hurling icy grains of sleet against the windows. Frigid drafts stole entrance around loose chinking and cast sprinkles of snow across the cold wood floors.

Warm and content, Alton slept, while Sue Ellen lay awake,

feeling her body grow clammy cold before the onslaught of the first searing white hot pain that was soon crashing over her in steady waves. Pain, like a relentless tide, ebbed and flowed. She drifted serenely for a few precious moments, then another swell of agony crested, leaving her gasping for breath.

The temperature plummeted. The cabin cooled.

Boosting herself from the straw tick, Sue Ellen staggered to the hearth, grunting as she rolled heavy logs into the grate. There was a spray of sparks as the fire caught, snapping and hissing with a comforting, cheerful sound. Soon the warmth engulfed Sue Ellen. She rocked and waited, the only sign of her pain the slack of her lips and the pinched whiteness of her knuckles clasping the arms of the rocker with each tumultuous upheaval.

"Sue! . . . *Sue!*"

Alton awoke with a start, blinking against the arrival of a glaring white dawn. He arose, pulled on his work clothes and boots, and looked out the window. Snow was swirling wildly across the meadow, driven by the breath of an icy wind that bent seasoned hardwood trees to their knees. Huge snow-drifts slanted across the lawn.

"Today?" he murmured when he saw Sue Ellen dozing near the hearth.

She nodded. "I think we'll have our Christmas babe, Alton—" Then another spasm gripped her, mercilessly clenching and squeezing, choking off her words.

"I'm going for Fanny," Alton announced.

"That might be best," Sue Ellen agreed. "I'd hoped we could wait a while so's not to intrude on Fanny's day and steal her from her family. But—"

"Horsefeathers, Sue!" Alton protested. "You're like family to Fanny Preston. And she'd be upset if I didn't fetch her in

76

plenty of time. The way that snow's comin' down, there's no time to lose."

Alton dressed warmly and went to the barn to hitch the team after giving Jeremiah instructions to stay with his mama and do her bidding.

"Heat water," Alton said. "An' keep the fire stoked."

"I'll take good care of her, Pa," Jem promised.

Alton ducked into the swirling snow, staggered through the drifts, and hauled himself into the seat of the buckboard. Hearing the snap of the reins, Doc and Dan moved out, their massive bodies swallowed up by the spiraling white flakes that blotted the world from view.

An hour went by. Then two.

Jem and Sue Ellen watched the hands of the ticking clock on the mantelpiece move forward in their relentless pace. She counted the minutes between the crushing pains that threatened to cleave her body in two, but the pains neither quickened nor slowed.

Jem fidgeted, stoked the fire, set the kettle of water on to boil, let it boil dry, filled the kettle again. Then he attacked the cabin with broom and feather duster, preferring woman's work to helpless waiting. Hearing a nicker of horses, Jem ran to the door.

"They're home, Ma!" Jem called, relief evident in his tone. "Pa and Fanny are coming up the lane."

When Fanny entered the cabin, she brought with her a good measure of confidence and cheer. Stomping the snow off her boots, she hovered near the hearth a moment, rubbing her chapped hands. Then pulling her scarf from her head, she shook it free of the wet snow that plopped to the floor, darkening the wood where it melted. All the while she kept up a steady flow of conversation.

"Oh, I'm so glad you're here, Fanny—" Sue Ellen gasped

77

in relief, "though I hated to take you from your family on this day."

"I was countin' on it, Sue Ellen Wheeler!" Fanny teased. "We've been prayin' for it since nigh onto early fall, haven't we? Once again the Lord has heard us. You're goin' to present Him—an' all of us—with a Christmas babe, my girl!"

"I hope so—"

Fanny gave her a sharp glance provoked by the bleakness of her words. "An' just how long have you been travailin', Sue?"

Sue Ellen closed her eyes wearily and tried to think. "The pains started during the night, Fanny. Near midnight, I'd guess."

Fanny nodded. "And how be the pains?" She listened intently as Sue Ellen explained the sequence.

"It appears this little one will be slow in coming," Sue Ellen said apologetically.

"Oh, I don't think so," Fanny disagreed. "Surely the Lord will grant arrival of the new babe by the stroke of midnight. This time tomorrow, honey, it will be all over and we'll have us a healthy, husky little rascal to love and spoil."

"Yes . . . ," Sue Ellen whispered weakly. Then, catching Fanny's spirit of optimism, her voice grew stronger. "*Yes!*"

"Now let's tuck you into bed," Fanny suggested, "and get down to work. I can't wait to see your young'un, Sue! Bet it'll be purty as a picture. What're you really hopin' for—boy or girl?"

"Whatever the Lord sends," Sue said softly.

"Bosh!" Fanny snorted. "Surely one would appeal a wee tad more'n the other."

"A boy, just like his pa," Sue Ellen admitted.

Fanny giggled. "I asked Alton the same question on the way over here—an' do you know what he said? 'A girl—jus' like her ma!'"

Sue Ellen tried to laugh, but just as Fanny was easing her into bed, another contraction took her breath, leaving her with only strength enough to moan.

"There, there, honey," Fanny said, patting her hand. "It'll pass. That's a good sign, now we're getting somewhere."

Fanny kept vigil, marveling at Sue Ellen's stoic endurance. A lesser woman would have howled in the throes of the birth pangs. But there was barely a whimper from the woman.

Alton camped near the doorway. Periodically he conferred with Fanny. At other times he listened to Sue Ellen's tortured sounds, praying as he never had before, that her time would pass quickly before *he* could endure no more.

"We'll have our child soon, Alton," Sue Ellen said at the stroke of six. "Go eat the nice meal Fanny has fixed. Surely it won't be long . . . now."

But the hours passed by.

Dusk gave way to inky dark, and a gentle snow hid the stars from sight.

The contractions strengthened and gripped Sue Ellen's body, breaking her, until her thin wails rent the stillness.

Fanchon clucked, fussed, and soothed, then wrung her hands in frustration and prayer when she escaped the birthing room to seek a moment's solace in the kitchen.

"If the weather weren't such a caution," Fanny confided to Alton, "I'd send you for the doctor. Maybe he—"

"What time is it, Fanny?" Sue Ellen's agonized question drew the stolid woman back to her side.

Fanny laid her hand on Sue Ellen's damp brow. The grandfather clock had gonged minutes before. "It's beyond the eleventh hour, Sue. But the Lord will give you all the time you need for bearin' this child."

"I know, Fanny," she sighed. "I don't doubt . . . His faithfulness. It's just that I'm so tired—"

She gripped the knotted bedsheet as her body contorted with pain. Racing the clock, Sue Ellen seemed to draw fresh resolve, and she met each vicious contraction with fierce determination of her own. Her throat grew raw, her voice hoarse from the screams she was now powerless to contain.

Tenderly Fanny spooned fresh snow to the agonized woman's lips, murmuring words of encouragement, praying for her quick release.

At Sue Ellen's first screams, Alton had cowered by the door, barely able to withstand the sound of his beloved wife's agony. Soon he could endure it no longer. Grabbing his heavy coat, he caught Fanny's eye.

Fanny nodded sympathetic permission and watched him go.

"Alton?" Sue Ellen murmured, sensing his absence. "Alton?"

"He's gone to the barn," Fanny soothed. "For just a moment—"

Sue Ellen's eyes sank shut. The dark circles surrounding her eyes and the hollowness of her cheeks gave her a ghostly countenance. Her lips moved in soft prayer, drawing from a wellspring deep within, new strength and courage.

"'Tis all for the best," Sue Ellen sighed, "because when he returns . . . I will have presented him with . . . our child!"

In all her years Fanchon Preston had never seen anything like it. She watched in awed fascination the determination and stamina of the slim woman. She feared that Sue Ellen would splinter apart. Reedy screams pierced the air, then hung, loud and wailing, to drape over them, enfolding them in guttural, velvety, raspy groans, that gave way to victorious pants.

"Fanny!" Sue Ellen gasped. "The baby's coming . . . it's coming!"

"Our Christmas babe is here at last!" Fanny cried. A

moment later Fanchon gave a great laugh as a welcome child's cry faintly greeted the world. "It's a girl, Sue Ellen Wheeler. A big, beautiful girl!"

"Oh . . . my little girl," Sue Ellen sighed and tears streamed down her cheeks. "Our little Mary—" she crooned.

"And what might be her middle name, dear?"

"Katharine," Sue Ellen whispered. "In honor of Alton's mama. I haven't asked him—but I'm sure he'll agree."

Alton's large frame suddenly filled the doorway.

"Judgin' by the look on his face, Sue Ellen, he heartily agrees." Fanny held up the infant, swaddled in clean linens. "Alton, your daughter."

He stared at the small, wrinkled creature, her hair soft and downy, but as black as his own and Sue Ellen's. Rounded cheeks, plump and smooth as little peaches, guarded a small nose, round as a cherry. Involuntarily he stepped back, awed by this tiny first fruit of their union.

"She won't break," Fanny assured him, nestling the warm bundle in his arms. "Take her to Sue Ellen for her mama to have a peek at our blessed Christmas babe."

The baby yowled. "The wee mite's hungry," Sue Ellen said.

Alton turned away as Fanny helped Sue Ellen place the infant to her breast.

"Play for me, Alton," Sue Ellen whispered. "Please play your harmonica."

He fetched it. "What would you like to hear, darlin'?" he asked tenderly.

Sue Ellen appeared too tired to answer.

"Bein' as it's Christmas, carols seem fittin', don't you think?" Fanny suggested.

The penetrating screams of the birthing had given way to the miracle of life, and serenity wrapped them in a quilt of comfort.

Alton drew in a breath, then blew it past the lump in his throat.

Silent night, Holy night . . .

The haunting strains swelled, wavering, then growing stronger, filling the cabin with joyous celebration.

Unexpectedly Sue Ellen's voice, surprisingly full for one so weak, joined the melody of Alton's harmonica. Together they made music, in worship, in thanksgiving, their thoughts in shared communion about the woman who so long ago had been obedient to the visitation of the Holy Spirit and had brought forth a child—a gift of healing redemption to all who would accept Him as Savior and Lord.

Alton's harmonica and Sue Ellen's voice trailed away, creating a silent night, a most holy night.

Alton stood mute with wonder, moved beyond speech, as he surveyed all that was his and counted his blessings. His wife was safe. His new daughter, healthy and whole. His prayers had been answered.

When he'd fled the screams of birthing to seek refuge in the barn, it had seemed fitting to kneel at one of the feeding troughs, a manger. As the animals gathered around, lending him their warmth, he'd begged deliverance for Sue Ellen, pleading the mercy of the One who had been born on this night so long ago.

By the time he returned to the cabin, his prayers had been answered.

But never again would he selfishly subject the woman he loved to such wretchedness!

Fanny rested on a pallet on the floor. Alton sat rigid in the rocker for long hours into the new morn. He threw fresh logs on the dying embers, then picked up the coal oil lamp and tiptoed into their bedroom where Sue Ellen slept and the baby nested beside her warm body.

82

Seeing her quiet as death, for a moment Alton feared that she was gone, until, mumbling in her sleep, Sue Ellen's head moved on the pillow and Alton's heart resumed its steady beat.

He left their bedroom to return to the rocking chair, but could not escape the recent memories that haunted him. Time and again his mind offered the clear, chilling vision of the pain, the torment, the bodily hell that Sue Ellen had bravely endured . . . because of him . . . because of his manly desire. The blame was his. And so was the guilt! They had their Mary Katharine—and Jem. A boy and a girl. Their cup of joy was full. No sacrifice was too great to safeguard that happiness forever.

Alton dropped his head into his clasped hands. This much he knew—he loved Sue Ellen too much to put her through such torture again. He would find the strength to resist his need for her—to conquer his love, his desire, that she might live in good health.

The strength was his to find and possess. Somewhere, somehow . . . he must find it. Oh, dear God, he *must!*

chapter
6

IT SEEMED TO Alton as if he'd scarcely fallen asleep in the rocker when the mewling cry of his daughter roused him. He jerked awake with a start.

Fanny had risen from the pallet and was already assisting Sue Ellen with the tiny babe. The crying subsided. Low murmurs hissed from the bedroom.

A moment later Fanny stepped from the room, holding her fingertip to her lips. "They're both doin' fine, thank the Lord," she whispered. Alton followed her to the kitchen. "Some women are made for bearin' babies . . . Sue Ellen ain't one o' them."

Even though he'd had no experience—being a bachelor until he'd found his Sue Ellen—he had discerned that her labor had been difficult, had come near to robbing her of her life, even as she bestowed the gift of life on their child.

"She'll be needin' to take her rest," Fanny pointed out. "I've made arrangements to stay on and be with you durin' Sue's confinement."

"We're much obliged to you, Fanny. Don't know what we'd 'a' done without your help," he croaked.

Fanchon sniffed and waved his words away as she vigorously stirred a pot of mush.

"She'd have done the same for me—or my Lizzie. I'm glad to be of help, Alton, an' would do it again, iffen there's ever a need." She frowned. "Though, to be honest, I'd rest much better with a doctor on hand next time."

Alton cleared his throat, considered the delicacy of the subject, then decided to speak candidly. "Won't be no 'next time,' Fanny," he said quietly. "Sue Ellen's not a young woman no more. If I'd had any notion what birthin' was like, I'd 'a' never put her through it—and won't again."

Fanny kept her back to Alton as she browned some side meat in a skillet on the wood range.

"Don't be too hard on yourself, Alton Wheeler," she suggested. "The Good Book says that women will bring forth babies in pain. An' . . . sometimes . . . for a gal like Sue, it's a worse pain to have her arms empty of the children she craves to hold and love than 'tis to bear a bit o' discomfort."

"But we have Mary Katharine now," Alton reasoned. "An', before we know it, Jeremiah will be sparkin' some gal in the neighborhood, weddin' her, and we'll have a passel of grandbabies to coddle 'n' spoil."

"O' course!" Fanny agreed brightly. "Sue Ellen can take comfort in that. Jem's a handsome lad, and, if I might be so cheeky as to say so, appealin' to the eye, with a polite, gentlemanly manner sure to turn the head of many a country gal."

The discussion ended when Jem emerged from the loft for breakfast.

Fanchon seated herself with the two men and hurriedly ate her meal before she prepared a tray for Sue Ellen. Almost immediately, she returned it to the kitchen, untouched.

"Reckon I'll let Sue Ellen sleep," she explained, as she poured boiling water into the dishpan and tossed in yellowish shavings of lye soap. "Right now she needs rest more'n she needs vittles."

Alton and Jem crept in to admire the tiny infant, then departed on tiptoe.

It was almost noon, and Alton had finished his chores outside in the blustery weather, when Sue Ellen awoke calling for him.

She gave him a tired but welcoming smile when he entered the small room. He felt a strange sense of shyness—as if he were an interloper. The baby's dark blue eyes moved in the direction of Alton's voice. He leaned over the bed and stroked her soft, tiny hand. Red and wrinkled the night before, by day her skin was creamy smooth.

"Ain't she a purty little thing?" Alton murmured, his words clutching in his throat. "I swear I've never seen such a purty babe, Sue!"

She beamed with pleasure. "I thought I felt that way because I'm her mother. But Fanny says so, too! Isn't Katie precious?"

"She is . . . 'n' so are you, Sue Ellen Wheeler," Alton said. Carefully he seated himself on the tick, being mindful not to jolt the bed. "I . . . I didn't realize exactly how precious until these last hours when I lived in raw fear of losin' you. You gave me a fright, you did. More than once last night I feared you weren't long for this world."

Sue Ellen patted his hand. "To be truthful, Alton, the thought crossed my mind, too," she admitted. "I'm just not as young as I once was."

"You still look it," Alton fibbed kindly, forcing himself not to see the gray pallor beneath her skin, or notice the new wrinkle on her brow, or how her eyes were darkened a hue with dullness borne of exhaustion. "You've never looked purtier to me, Sue."

Sue Ellen gave him a weak grin and drew his strong hand to her lips.

"Shame on you, Alton Wheeler," she teased. For a moment her eyes danced. "Scarcely have I presented you with one strapping young'un than you start plying me with pretty words, wooing me all over again."

Intended to tease, the joke fell flat for Alton, and instead served as a heightened reminder of his promise to himself, made in the wee hours the night before.

"I'll be beggin' your pardon, then, Sue Ellen Wheeler. You've already given me more'n a man could desire. I won't be askin' of you more'n you should give."

Sue Ellen frowned at the seriousness in his tone and regarded him with puzzlement. But when he gave her a boyish grin and quickly kissed her cheek, she cast aside her contemplations.

When Fanny arrived with a basin of hot water, linens, soft soap, and toiletries, Alton found himself strangely relieved to escape the room where he suddenly felt edgy and on guard.

Fanny remained the rest of that week and into the next. By then Jem and Alton were capable of seeing to Sue Ellen and the baby during the day and, at night, the cradle was placed close to Sue Ellen's bed.

One day gave way to another, fast becoming weeks, then months.

Mary Katharine, soon called Katie by the family, was the delight of the household. She possessed a happy, sunny nature, cried little, and was seldom troubled with colic. Katie grew plump and healthy as quickly as Sue Ellen was slow to regain her health.

By April Alton was concerned with her continuing pallor. She laughed away his concerns and refused to seek more rest.

"If you had your way, Alton Wheeler," Sue Ellen protested as she prepared a special feast to commemorate the anniversary of their marriage, "you'd have me lying abed day and night. Of course I'm weak," she admitted, "but how's a body to gain strength? A bit of work won't hurt me. It's coddling I don't need." Teasing softened her tone. "But your daughter thrives on it." Then she deposited the solid baby in Alton's arms and turned back to her work.

As if prophetic, Sue Ellen's words proved true, to Alton's great relief. Day by day he began to witness the return of her old strength and vigor. Fresh color rose in her cheeks as the active baby grew older and less demanding, allowing Sue Ellen more restful nights.

When Alton left his pallet near the hearth to return to Sue Ellen's bed a month after Katie was born, the transition was made with fear and trepidation on his part.

What would he do if Sue Ellen reached for him in the night? Would his resolve crumble like the walls of Jericho? Would he find the words to explain—in a genteel manner—that he cherished and loved her so much that he could be satisfied with a chaste kiss rather than risk the danger that accompanied passion?

But as the months passed, Alton found no need for his carefully rehearsed speeches.

Alton convinced himself that, just as he had reached a decision for a chaste marriage as described in Scripture, Sue Ellen, too, had come to a similar conclusion after her terrifying ordeal. No doubt she was grateful that he hadn't reduced her to flushing, stammering, and a need to draw out painful, mortifying details in order to gain his understanding and cooperation.

But Alton, firmly convinced he was right, failed to notice the confused, mystifying glances Sue Ellen surreptitiously cast his way. Neither did he recognize the hurt longing in her eyes when she'd impulsively put her arms around him and he, fearing that his love for her would call for more restraint than he possessed, found excuse to break away. Turning away from her at such times, Alton was unaware that Sue Ellen's heart was weeping while her eyes and lips smiled on.

She recalled the early months of their marriage when Alton had drowned her in his love and affection. Comparing his earlier passion with the cool detachment of their present relationship, Sue Ellen pondered the change.

Time and again throughout the day she wandered to her room, and, mesmerized, stared into the hazy mirror on her bedroom wall. Her green eyes sadly studied her reflection, and she wondered if she had grown so unattractive that her own husband no longer desired her as his wife.

By the time Katie took her first halting steps, Sue Ellen's wounded pride gave way to her longing.

One autumn evening Alton routinely prepared to retire, seemingly unaware that Sue Ellen had taken special pains to make herself pretty before she joined him.

No sooner had he blown out the lamp than she slipped between the crisp sheets. When she snuggled against him, Alton's heart galloped to a wild cadence beneath her ear. He swallowed hard.

"Shuckydarn, but I'm tired," Alton yawned pointedly.

Silence thickened in the room—so intense that it seemed to crackle and snap like the sparks in the fireplace.

"*Tired?*" Sue Ellen spat the words. Then her voice crescendoed to become a harsh grating rasp. "Tired from your work . . . or tired of me as your wife?"

The horrible question hung in the air, punctuated by

90

gasping sobs as Sue Ellen collapsed to the tick, until the bed shook from the force of her unhappiness. Dazed, wretchedly confused, Alton bolted upright. The world seemed to reel around him.

He knew that he should reach out and comfort Sue Ellen, allay her fears with sweet words, but he feared that the silken warmth of her flesh beneath the rough calluses of his palms would provoke more than he had the strength to withstand.

Each second spiraled into an eternity.

Alton had never seen Sue Ellen weep and carry on so, not even in the throes of childbirth. He was sick with the grief he'd caused her, but if only she understood how difficult it had been for *him*. If only she knew that it was his great love for her—and for the Lord—that had allowed him to live so chastely when the slightest casual movement, impish smile as she whisked hair from her face, or bent to scratch a chigger bite on her ankle, made him want her all the more until the desire was all but overpowering.

"Sue . . . darlin', I—I ain't tired of you," Alton's stammered speech rumbled in the darkness.

He moved to reassure her. But Sue Ellen flinched, recoiling at his touch. She jerked her bare shoulder away from further chance contact, huddling on her own side of the tick as if she couldn't remove herself far enough from him.

"For not being tired of me, Alton Wheeler, you've surely put on a fine act," she hissed. Her voice cracked and became wet and squeaky with tears. She sprang up in bed. "H—how do you think I've felt all these months . . . having you draw away from me as if I were unclean? *Hurt!* That's how I've felt. It's a special pain to know that my husband no longer finds me appealing. If you don't want me as your wife, why don't you just put me away from you and move on, Alton?" She paused. "I'll live . . . I've done it before."

Alton was stricken by her suggestion.

"Mebbe you'd live, Sue Ellen Wheeler, but as for me, I'd surely die," he said. "You're wrong, Sue darlin'—so wrong in thinkin' I don't desire you!" He groaned. "If only you knew how many nights I've laid awake wantin' you but afraid to make you mine. I just couldn't—"

"*Couldn't?*" Her voice was a breathy plea. "Or . . . *wouldn't?*"

Alton felt the weight of her words descend on him. "Both," he whispered.

"Couldn't? Wouldn't?" Sue Ellen choked on the revelation. "But . . . why?"

"Because I loved you too much."

"Loved me too much?" Sue Ellen repeated, laughing lightly, although the sound was heavy with bitter sarcasm. "Since Mary Katharine was born, you haven't loved me enough. *You haven't loved me at all*—"

Alton was afraid to reach out to her, for fear she'd shrink away again. "Not because I haven't wanted to, Sue," he admitted softly.

Sue Ellen was brazen in her outrage. "If you've wanted to so badly," she pointed out, "then why haven't you?"

"Because I won't risk your gettin' in the family way again. The young'uns need you . . . 'n' I need you, too. I can't risk possessin' you for a few blissful nights only to lose you forever."

Sue Ellen was silent. But only for a moment. "All you cared about was yourself, Alton Wheeler," she accused in a low tone. "You might have at least discussed your decision with me before you took to shunning me as your wife."

"I didn't want to risk offense, Sue, discussin' such things. Rememberin' your birthin' screams, I reckoned maybe you'd figgered it best, too—"

"Alton, Alton—" Sue Ellen moaned softly, her anger dissipating in the face of his clumsy, loving intentions. "The Good Book says that a man and woman should leave their parents to cleave to each other and become one in spirit and in flesh. The Lord means for us to live as man and wife. The Bible says it's not right for a husband and wife to deny each other except when they both agree for a time. You've no more right to deny me of your husbandly love than I'd have in rejecting you."

"Yes . . . but—" Alton struggled miserably.

"There's a season for all things, Alton. A time to be born, a time to die, a time to blossom, a time to wither, a time to rejoice, a time to weep. For women, there are seasons, too."

"Sue—," Alton murmured against the corner of her mouth. Their lips met, clung, then he broke away, hesitant.

"Trust me, Alton," she whispered.

Sue Ellen's lips yielded to Alton's, her arms met and returned his embrace. After the long months of waiting, with passion unrestrained, they celebrated anew the miracle of marriage.

The seasons came and went.

Balmy spring breezes replaced winter's icy blast, and were themselves driven away by the hot breath of summer. Then came the bite of autumn, heralding winter's frigid storms. And so the cycle of life continued.

Trusting Sue Ellen's intuitions, Alton labored by day and sought solace in her loving arms by night. His faith was rewarded as one year passed, followed by another in which his Sue grew more beautiful and desirable than she had ever been in her younger years. There was a new softness and serenity born of contentment that wrenched his heart each time he looked at her.

Alton was in the springtime of his thirty-seventh year, with Sue Ellen not far behind, and Katie, almost three, when Jeremiah reached his seventeenth birthday. The event was marked with an elaborate cake of Sue Ellen's creation.

"Mmmmm, good, if I do say so myself," she commented, daintily licking frosting from her fingertip.

"You may as well," Alton said. "Everyone else has!" He held out his plate to accept a second wedge of cake. Sue Ellen deftly deposited a thin slice on her own plate, too.

"If I don't quit taking second helpings," she admonished herself, "I'm going to be as matronly as Fanny! What an appetite I have these days!"

Alton shrugged. "I like seein' a woman eat hearty. You won't find me complainin'—there'll be just that much more of you to love." He cast a fond glance at Sue Ellen. "Surely you didn't expect to stay a slim slip forever, did you? Why, Jem's old enough to go courtin'. Maybe a year or two from now, some gal will reel him in and we'll be dandlin' some of their young'uns on our knee. I'd say it's 'bout time you was lookin' like a granny."

But he knew he was a liar. Sue Ellen had never looked better. There was a youthful glow that reminded him of the early days of their own courtship.

"Well . . . I—"

Suddenly she seemed strangely without words and suffered an immediate loss of appetite. Hurriedly she swept up her plate, the cake unfinished, and busied herself in the kitchen.

Later Jem went calling on the Nash family across Bishop Creek, and Alton whittled a toy for Katie while Sue Ellen mended an apron. The atmosphere in the cozy cabin was peaceful and intimate. Sue Ellen sighed. She just couldn't bring herself to force the difficult words past her lips. Maybe later—

Before readying for bed she crossed to the trundle to peer down at Katie, who was sleeping soundly, her thumb hooked into her mouth, her finger cupping her small nose. Sue Ellen's heart swelled with love so powerful it was like sweet pain in her chest.

Instinctively her hands went to her waist, thickening already, enough so that even Alton had been noticing and joshing her about growing plump. She glanced into the mirror. Her face had filled out, too. And there was a glow in her eyes reflecting the light of her happiness within. But it faded a bit when she considered Alton's reaction to the news she must find a way to share with him.

Already she'd kept her secret long weeks. Throughout the quiet evening spent with Alton after Jeremiah's departure, the words had been just out of reach of the tip of her tongue. Oh, how she wished she could have unburdened her heart! But she had dreaded his knowing, dreaded the worry this new blessing would cause him.

Sue Ellen turned down the coverlet, then straightened, rubbing her tired back that ached already from the increasing weight she was carrying.

When she heard Alton's tread on the wood floor across the threshold, she forced herself upright and faced him with a bright smile. He answered it with a weary one of his own. Yawning, he seated himself on the tick and pulled off his boots.

"I'm plumb tuckered, woman," he said, yawning again. "I'm gettin' too old for this foolishness, it seems. If it's right what the Good Book says—that man earns his bread by the sweat of his brow—then Jem an' I sure did today!" He shook his head in rueful amusement. "An' him spry enough to go sparkin' a purty girl tonight!"

"Shall I fetch the liniment?" Sue Ellen asked with concern.

Alton shook his head. "Don't trouble yourself. I 'spect you're as tired as I be."

Alton snuggled beneath the thick coverlets, letting out a long sigh of contentment. Sue Ellen stayed up to brush her hair, the words she sought still eluding her. When she slipped between the chilly sheets, Alton was already asleep and the opportunity had fled.

With the first rays of dawn, and Katie's whimpers shortly thereafter, Sue Ellen began her day. Although the mere smell of the jowl frying in the cast-iron spider turned her stomach, she doggedly kept up her preparations for a hearty breakfast. *Alton and Jem needed food and a lot of it to keep up their strength,* she thought, ignoring the tiny beads of perspiration that dotted her upper lip.

Sue Ellen seated herself long enough to share table grace with the family. She took a sip of steaming coffee and managed a bite of toast dripping with peach marmalade before her entire being revolted, and the room began to sway and spin around her.

She rose abruptly, a quaking smile on her lips. "Tomato juice will go nicely with breakfast," she excused herself, darting from the room to exit the cabin in the direction of the cellar.

Scarcely had she escaped the confines of the hot kitchen, permeated with disturbing odors, than Sue Ellen was overtaken by waves of nausea.

Gasping for breath, she clasped the hem of her skirts and scurried to seek privacy behind the weather-beaten shed. There she retched until she was faint from the exertion and tears ran freely. Spent, she leaned against the clapboard shed, panting, as she willed the nausea to pass.

When it did, she stood upright and took a few steps toward

the cabin. But the undulating sensations returned in force, leaving her shivering and shaking.

"Sue!"

Weak with her retching, she was helpless to answer Alton's summons and didn't want to.

"Sue?!" Alton called again.

She held her silence and soon heard him enter the shed, cross the floor with heavy steps, and throw the trap door open with a bang. An instant later, not finding her, he emerged, bellowing her name again.

Sue Ellen felt too frightened and ill to answer. One look at her—and Alton would guess her secret.

"*Sue!*" Alton screamed, his voice cracking.

"I—I'm right h—here, Alton," Sue Ellen stuttered.

Alton was behind the shed instantly, in time to catch her quickly dabbing at her eyes and the corner of her lips. She straightened up, her eyes haunted and hollow.

His knees seemed to melt with relief. "You gave me a scare. I thought you'd fallen down the cellar steps—"

"I'm all right," Sue Ellen said, managing a faltering smile.

Alton studied her. "You're sickly this mornin', ain't you? Are you ill enough to be needin' a doctor?"

"Yes. No. Well, not really . . . sick," she said. "Just a mite puny today. There's no need to send for a doctor. At least, not yet."

Alton stared. One by one the isolated hints fell into place, and he knew. His face drained of color.

"You're in the family way again, ain't you?"

Sue Ellen gave a quick nod, then burst into tears. "Yes! Yes, I am. Alton, oh please don't be angry. And don't be scared. Be happy . . . for me . . . for us."

Alton clutched to support himself against the sturdy shed as the weight of the moment crushed him beneath the immen-

97

sity of its meaning. He shivered. Echoing from the past came the memory of Sue Ellen's tortured groans and ear-splitting shrieks. He cursed himself for what he had done to her. Again. He should have kept his vow . . . should have insisted—

"Please be happy, Alton. For my sake, be happy."

He looked at Sue Ellen with a dazed, hollow stare. "Oh, I am, darlin', I am!" But he spoke too quickly, too enthusiastically, and she was not convinced.

Alton clasped her to him, drying her tears. "I'm happy, Sue Ellen," he said, this time with conviction. "A mite surprised, too, I must admit, since you've already given me so much. And, well, after what we decided—"

"What we decided counts little," Sue Ellen said serenely. "It's what the Lord desires that matters. He'll help me in my hour of need, Alton. We can trust Him for that. This is His will, so it's best that we accept it gladly."

"Yes," Alton said. "We'll make arrangements for a doctor to be on hand this time . . . make sure he can get here . . . though I 'spect Fanny Preston will count on helpin' out, too."

"We can be sure of it," Sue Ellen said, feeling a sudden bubble of happiness now that her news was out and they were facing the event together.

"It's time you started takin' life a bit easier." Alton's tone brooked no argument. "Jem 'n' I will help out. An' I want no sass nor complaints from you, woman. You've always pampered us, now it's our turn to return the favor."

Sue Ellen leaned into the circle of Alton's arm around her shoulders and wiped a furtive tear. "I love you so much, Alton Wheeler. What would I ever do without you?"

Alton's lips fell to her cheek, then trailed to her mouth, effectively silencing her before she could pose the tormenting question again.

Then, a question so poignant, so frightening, so hideous took root in his imagination, creating a specter so horrible, that he couldn't bring himself to contemplate it, let alone give it utterance. Though he tried to banish the thought, it begged release, dancing and leaping through his tortured mind.

God, oh dear God, what would I ever do without Sue Ellen?

chapter
7

JUST AS HE had promised, Alton labored to make Sue Ellen's life easier. In the Wheeler cabin there was no woman's work—only tasks to be accomplished—and Alton viewed them as his and Jem's to share.

Although Sue Ellen kept her spirits high and forced smiles that shielded the men in her family from her inner agony, Fanny Preston was not deceived.

"I'll be glad for September to arrive, and this babe of yours with it," Fanny admitted one day when she came to visit Sue Ellen and enjoy a cup of tea. Nearby Katie played with the cornhusk doll Fanny had crafted for her.

Sue Ellen seated herself heavily. "That will make two of us, Fanny," she agreed.

The older woman studied Sue Ellen. "You're not feelin' too pert, are you?"

As if she wanted to deny it but knew better than to try to fool Fanchon Preston, Sue Ellen settled for a quick shake of her head.

"You and my Lizzie could be havin' a race," Fanny changed the direction of the conversation. "Just last week she told me she and her Harmon are goin' to present us with a new grandbaby. I kind of suspected it, though, before she confided in her old ma. It seems gals in the family way have a twinklin' about the eyes. . . . It gives 'em away 'most ever' time."

Sue Ellen smiled, but the effort failed to reach her tired eyes. She made no comment and took a sip of her tea.

"Exceptin' you, Sue Ellen Wheeler," Fanny said, frowning. "I swear the circles under your eyes look dark as chimney soot ever' time I see you. You'd best be gettin' more rest, gal!"

Sue Ellen sighed. "That's all I hear."

Fanny leaned back in her chair and slipped her arm around Katie as the tot crowded close. "Well, I'm glad to hear it," Fanny remarked. "Just hope you're heedin' the advice. You're not a young gal anymore. Carryin' and bearin' a child takes the starch out of a woman. Even those that seem made for havin' babies . . . which you ain't."

Sue Ellen's lifted her chin. "I'll be fine . . . just fine," she said stiffly.

"O' course you will," Fanny assured. "The doc . . . an' I . . . we'll see to that."

"You'll probably have your work cut out for you, tending your Lizzie," Sue Ellen reminded her.

Fanny gave a wave of her hand. "Oh, I've got plenty o' time for the both o' you. Lizzie's not due for a long spell. An', as big as you're gettin', Sue, wouldn't be surprised if you bear that young'un sooner than you think. Unless I miss my guess," she said, eying the bloated body of her friend, "it's either goin' to be a strappin' youngster like its pa . . . or twins."

Sue Ellen paled, laughed, then realized that Fanny was not bantering.

"Well, twins would put me ahead of your Lizzie, Fanny," Sue Ellen teased lightly when she recovered from the idea.

Fanny chuckled. "Just wait 'til I tell her you said that!

102

SEASONS OF THE HEART

Better yet, tell her yourself when we all get together for a picnic to celebrate our independence on the Fourth of July."

"I'll send Alton, Jem, and Katie," Sue Ellen promised. "That is, if I don't feel well enough myself to attend."

"Try to come, Sue," Fanny encouraged. "'Twould do you good to have a little fun for a change."

On the Fourth of July Sue Ellen awakened with the best of intentions. She scurried around to prepare a hamper brimming with special culinary delights—all of Alton's favorites. But by the time that he had hitched the team, and Jem had slicked himself up, conquering his rebellious cowlick, Sue Ellen was miserable. Her feet were so swollen she could scarcely wedge them into her shoes. And when Katie whined and stamped her foot when Sue Ellen tried to brush her tangled hair into a dark halo around her cherubic face, it was the last straw!

"Drat!" Sue Ellen gave vent to frustration, slamming the hairbrush to the dresser. Tears welled in her eyes.

When the bewildered child gazed up into her mother's face, Sue Ellen impulsively crushed Katie to her, burrowing her face in Katie's soft curls.

"Somethin' troublin' you, Sue?" Alton asked when he found them thus.

Sue Ellen shook her head, then nodded reluctantly. "I'm tired," she murmured. "More tired than I've ever been in my life. You, Jem, and Katie . . . go to the celebration . . . and leave me here alone."

"Now, Sue—," Alton began his protest, then seeing the plea in her eyes, he quickly conceded. "We'll go, but I'll be comin' home to check on you a time or two durin' the afternoon."

"There's no call to do that. I'll be just fine . . . as soon as I get some rest."

"Mebbe ain't no call," Alton murmured under his breath, "but I'll be back anyhow."

Without Sue Ellen, the celebration had little of the sparkle and spontaneity of others in the past. Helplessly his thoughts spiraled back to their first Fourth of July celebration together when the neighbors had gathered for Harmon and Lizzie's barn raising and stayed on to picnic and party long into the summery night.

Sue Ellen had looked so pretty it had made his head swim. Even now, years later, Alton felt himself prickle with discomfort when he recalled the tense confrontation between them at the hoedown, and how he'd been so emboldened by the music and the approving glints in the neighbors' eyes that he'd openly courted Sue Ellen though she was not long enough a widow.

A chill zigzagged through Alton when he considered the morrow and realized that it would mark the date when he'd left Sue Ellen's farm, striking his own declaration of independence from the influence of her Christian love. He'd driven the team away that day, not even waving to Will Preston as he left the area, contenting himself with the mistaken notion that he was free of Sue Ellen Stone. Free of the chance for further hurt. Free of her godly ways and restrictions. But he'd been a prisoner of her love, helplessly fettered by feelings that had seemed to know no human bounds.

"C'mon, Alton!" A friend broke through his reminiscences. "Leave your young'un with the womenfolk and come pitch horseshoes!"

Cajoled into taking part, Alton deposited Katie with a willing Lizzie and joined the men.

Only when a number of games had been played did Alton

find a moment to slip away and return home. There was no sign of life when he entered the quiet homestead. He halted the team and stealthily walked to the cabin, entering noiselessly.

Sue Ellen was in bed—so still that for a moment Alton's heart almost stopped beating. What if she was dead, passed from this life alone, without her loved ones gathered around? Just as he was about to sob out his wild grief, she moved, and he felt joyous relief. With thanksgiving in his heart, he left as quietly as he had come, hoping she could sleep the afternoon away.

"How's Sue?" Fanny asked, when he rejoined the celebrants.

Alton shook his head sadly. "Plumb tuckered. She was layin' abed an' didn't even wake when I looked in on her. She was so quiet she gave me a scare."

"Rest is what she needs," Fanny nodded. "'Tis the best thing for her."

"And rest is what she'll get," Alton vowed.

From that day forward, Alton ordered Sue Ellen to her bed almost every chance he got. At first she made token protest, but soon, he noticed, she agreed with grateful acquiescence.

With Fanny's help and some from Lizzie, who bloomed with health as her body blossomed with child, Alton and Jeremiah put by vegetables for the winter, while Sue Ellen rocked Katie and looked on, too weak to object, too frail to take part.

In the last month of her confinement, the look of pain was ever present on Sue Ellen's face and she could scarcely bear to stir from her bed.

"Twins," Fanny pronounced the verdict with somber

finality. She shook her head in doleful acceptance. "Twins . . . an' with her so wee and weak."

September arrived and, with it, the early fall rains. Between chilly showers, full ears of corn hung from the drying stalks as papery leaves rattled in the brisk wind. For days the rain fell, sending rivulets of cold water trickling over the earth, then rushing downhill, eventually draining into the creeks and overflowing their banks to spill over the bottom lands, flooding fields and drowning the trails.

"Send for Fanny," Sue Ellen murmured one morning, around the middle of September, when Alton awoke for the day. "Please send for Fanny."

Alton threw on his clothes, roused Jeremiah, and was ready to depart in minutes. Needles of rain still slanted from the leaden sky.

"After I alert Fanchon," Alton told her, "I'll go for the doctor."

Sue Ellen gave a weak laugh. "It will do no good, Alton."

"'Course it will, darlin'!" Alton assured stoutly, loath to believe she might be right. "Fanny's plenty good—but doctors—well, they know things midwives don't."

Sue Ellen shook her head. "He won't come . . . can't come . . . The creeks . . . it's been raining for days, you know that," she murmured. "The Little Wabash River, and Salt and Bishop Creeks have been flooded all week." A groan overtook her. "You can't get to him—"

"I *will* get to him!" Alton cried. "And I . . . I'll bring him back! I'll find a boat!" he promised rashly, casting about for a solution, however far-fetched.

Dropping a kiss on her brow, he made for Fanny's place, lashing the whip above the heads of his faithful horses. Though the trail was treacherous underfoot, he reached the Preston farm to find Fanny already packed and ready to leave.

On the way back he laid out his plan. "We'll have a doctor," Alton vowed, "if I have to hogtie him and float him over the river on my own back!"

"That's a relief, Alton," Fanny admitted. "I don't mind tellin' you, I'd a been afeared to try to bring those babes into the world 'thout help."

Depositing Fanny and her belongings in the cabin, where Jem was sponging Sue Ellen's face with cool water, Alton took his leave once more.

"Go . . . and Godspeed!" Fanny murmured, glancing at the tortured woman on the bed.

Thus began a nightmarish day for Alton. A driven man, he guided the team along soggy country roads. The wagon slipped, skidded, and balked up the hills, then careened and slid on the downside, threatening to overturn.

Unable to obtain a boat at any of the farms where he stopped to inquire, Alton found one fellow sensitive to his plight. The farmer offered a raft, used for fishing, then helped to load it onto the wagon. If a boat could not be found, this crude affair might allow passage across the swollen creek.

By the time Alton reached the bank of the creek, the small tributary that was generally little more than a trickle had engorged to include an area a half a mile in radius, swallowing everything in its path from hillside to hillside. Trees jutted crazily from the murky water, the dampness of their bark marking the depth of the flood waters, visible evidence of Alton's dilemma.

Grunting, he hauled the raft from the wagon. It toppled with a thud at his feet. Straining until he cried out from the effort and frustration, he inched the cumbersome log structure toward the swirling current.

Carefully securing the horses for the long wait, Alton nudged the raft into the water and leaped on, thinking to grab a pole only at the last minute. But once the rude craft was captured by the swift-moving current, the pole did little good, and Alton found himself helplessly sucked downstream, alternately cursing the delay and praying for deliverance.

When he landed at the other side, he banked the raft, then scurried up the wet, slippery hillside. He ran as he had never run before, but another precious hour had ticked by before he arrived on the stoop of the doctor's neat residence in the small village. He battered on the door, then sagged against the clapboards, gasping for breath.

It seemed forever before the door was opened, and then, Alton realized with a sinking heart, by a slow-witted servant girl instead of the doctor. Rage battled with frustrated despair when the buxom lass, who spoke only German and understood almost none of what he said, shrugged and rolled her eyes. Frightened by his desperation, she shut the door in his face.

It was then that one of the doctor's neighbors, overhearing the exchange, called out: "The doc's not in! Went to do surgery days ago, but the rains caught him unawares. . . . There's three creeks to cross 'tween us an' him."

"Then there's—" Alton couldn't finish the thought.

There was to be no help for his Sue Ellen. No one but Fanny and, he added with a shrinking faith, the Lord.

Wasting no more time, Alton sprinted for the creek. He ran with single-minded purpose, tormenting himself with the image of the raft escaping, leaving him stranded, unable to swim the breadth of the deep, fast-moving stream.

But the raft was where he had secured it, and he leaped aboard and began the dizzying journey to the other side. He landed downstream, then hauled the raft upriver to where the team waited patiently.

Panting for breath, Alton played out the length of rope on

the back of the wagon as the team hauled the raft up the incline. Then with his last ounce of strength, he wrestled it aboard before collapsing, soaked to the skin and shivering with the cold.

But he was too worried about Sue Ellen to be concerned about dry clothing, and he grasped the edges of the spring seat to maintain balance as the wagon jounced over the slick clay roads. He paused only long enough to return the raft to its owner before he was on his way again to his Sue.

Fanny heard his arrival, as did Jeremiah, and they rushed to the cabin door expectantly. They were unable to camouflage their disappointment when they saw Alton's lone presence. In a numb tone he delivered the news.

"If we were meant to have a doctor," Fanny murmured acceptingly, "then He'd have provided us one. We'll just trust in Him to give us the knowledge and wisdom as we have need."

Alton nodded weakly, unconvinced. Even Fanny, who had an unshakable faith, seemed jolted by this latest turn of events.

Though Alton's perilous journey in search of help had seemed torturous, he would come to believe that fighting the devilish currents had been child's play compared to the horror that awaited him in the cabin.

"One of the twins is in breech," Fanny explained. "But it's to be expected, her bearin' two babies. The presentation is bad. She's been laborin' hard, since you left, and 'taint accomplishin' nary a thing."

Sue Ellen was out of her head with pain. Screams competed with sobs, and Fanny's cries mingled with those of her young friend. The misery seemed endless, and minutes dragged by like hours.

Alton was grateful when choring time arrived so he could

escape the hideous sounds. But even as he moved through the autumn rain, carrying out his tasks by rote, the screams echoed in his mind, leaving him unsure as to whether he was hearing the rumble of thunder or the reality of the agony carrying from the cabin on the night air.

Hours later, desperate prayer on her lips as she cried out to God for help, Fanny pulled the babes—first one, then the other—into the world.

Instantly Sue Ellen's screams died away, giving birth to blessed silence, disturbed only by the infants' indignant squalls in being wrested so unceremoniously from their dark sanctuary.

Dazed, Alton confronted the babies—twin girls—and was drained of further emotion.

Fanny sponged the babies and wrapped them in fresh flannel before she brought them near the hearth for Alton's inspection.

She tucked the twins into the cradle Katie had long since outgrown, then turned to Alton, motioning him to the kitchen.

"I sent Jeremiah to Lizzie's to fetch Katie home so's she can see her mama," Fanny murmured. Alton nodded.

"I'm sure glad it's over," he whispered, misunderstanding. "Don't know how Sue could have stood much more—or me, either, for that matter."

Fanny's eyes filled with tears. "It ain't over, Alton. Sue's not goin' to make it. I'm hopin' that Jem gets here with Katie so's Sue can see her lil' one before she departs this life."

"N—n—not going to make it?" Alton stammered in horror.

Fanny nodded, resigned. "She knows. I expected it, but didn't say nothin'. Sue told me herself that she's not long for this earth."

Alton began to cry, brokenly, burying his head in his hands.

"Our days are numbered from the moment we're born, Alton. Her time has come," Fanny said firmly, "and she's ready to meet her Lord. And, Alton Wheeler, you're goin' to face Sue Ellen like a brave Christian man. Don't you trouble her dyin' moments with cursin', ragin' and bellerin' like you used to do. Do you understand, Alton?"

"Fanny, no. . . ." Alton whimpered. "I can't! Oh . . . please—"

"She don't have much longer," Fanny cautioned. "Now go . . . comfort her. Tell her your last words and hear hers." With a gentle shove she propelled him toward the doorway shielded by a heavy curtain.

The journey from the kitchen to the bedroom was the longest of Alton's life; the destination, the one he had feared most since taking Sue Ellen as his wife. As he trod the short distance he prepared himself for the worst, but what confronted him brought a cry of anguish from the depths of his soul.

At the sound, Sue Ellen forced her eyes open. She was drained of life, and her eyes seemed overly large in her wan, pinched face. She managed a serene smile through cracked lips and beckoned Alton to her bedside.

"Sue . . . oh, Sue, darlin'!" Alton sobbed.

He knelt beside the bed. Sue Ellen's frail hand folded gentle as a mourning dove's wing over his heaving shoulder.

"It's the Lord's will," Sue Ellen said in a faint voice. "I'm so tired, so tired . . . but rest will be mine, Alton. What remains for you . . . is to raise our little ones. . . . Fanny's promised to help . . . and Lizzie."

"Sue, don't go! Don't leave me!" Alton begged.

Sue Ellen sighed. "That promise isn't . . . mine to give,

Alton," she whispered sadly. "But before I go, I'd be comforted . . . if you'd promise *me* . . . something."

"Yes, yes, anything!" Alton said rashly, holding Sue Ellen close. Her form yielded to his, unresisting as a rag doll, and he was unaware of the pain in her eyes as he embraced her.

She swallowed hard and licked her dry lips. "Raise up my son and our little girls . . . in the faith, Alton. . . . No sacrifice is too dear. . . . Never let them know . . . you sometimes doubt His loving care."

"With God's help," Alton vowed, crying softly. "Yes—"

"One thing more . . ." Alton bent near to hear the weakening whisper. "You must love again, Alton."

Alton recoiled from the very thought. With his beloved Sue Ellen dying in his arms, it seemed an affront to his love for her, an indecency, that she should ask him—*make him promise*—to love and cherish another.

"No!" Alton cried.

In a babble of words he expressed his feelings for Sue Ellen, saying even the things he couldn't have brought himself to utter had moments not been fast spinning away toward eternity, leaving him behind.

"I can't love another woman, Sue. You're my heart, my love, my very life. Don't ask me! Compared to you—"

"There will be no comparisons," Sue Ellen broke in to whisper the soft command. "The Lord will provide . . . a new love, Alton. . . . Don't resist like you once retreated from my love . . . and God's. . . . Promise me . . . ," she said, weakening. "Promise me, Alton, . . . that you'll love again. . . . Our little girls will need . . . a mama."

Further protests tumbled to Alton's lips, flowing forth as life ebbed from Sue Ellen's body.

Suddenly the pain in his heart lessened, if only by the

excruciating agony that struck his ankle and shot to the thigh, leaving a dull throb.

Without having to look, Alton knew that Fanchon had tiptoed into the room and overheard Sue's request. Sue Ellen repeated her desire. Again, Alton hesitated but only for a moment when he noticed movement and saw Fanny lift her brogan from the wood floor.

"Promise me . . . ," Sue Ellen coaxed, sighing. "You never broke a promise to me. . . . Let me die holding you to . . . the honor of your word."

Fanchon gave Alton a stern glare. "I promise . . . I'll love again . . . but only if it's the Lord's will," Alton amended his vow.

Fanny slowly replaced her foot to the floor, satisfied.

Sue Ellen smiled hazily into his eyes and swallowed her own tears. "I love you, Alton. . . . And tell our children . . . now and . . . always—"

"Sue, they're—"

Alton tried to tell her that Jeremiah was on his way back, that Katie was with him, only moments away. But time ceased to exist, the world stood still, and before his eyes Alton witnessed his beloved wife depart on a path he could not yet follow. She brushed his arm with the touch of a feather drifting in the wind, then her hand slid limply to her side. *She was gone.*

Deep racking sobs erupted from the depths of Alton's being, rending him the length and breadth of his body and leaving no part of him unravaged. He stayed thus for a long time, not wanting to leave Sue Ellen's lifeless form, until he was spent.

Alton stumbled from the cabin, dodging Fanny, who carried soap, a basin of water, salty brine, pennies, and linens with which to lay out the dead.

113

Alton staggered outside and fell against a tree, clutching it as he had once embraced Sue Ellen, sobbing his grief against its harsh, rough bark.

"Pa!" Jem cried, shaken, when he saw Alton. "Oh, Pa— no!" Jem's own sobs began and blindly he raced into the cabin, his wail further breaking Alton's heart. "Mama! Mama!" Jem blubbered brokenly. Wordlessly, Katie clung to Alton's legs, silent in her confusion.

Alton's eyes were red and gritty from tears. He felt drained when Fanny approached him.

"Will's got a nice walnut coffin in the shed," she told him as gently as possible. "We keep one on hand for the neighbor- hood . . . for times like this. It's your'n if you want it an' don't have time to build one, what with Katie, an' the twins."

Alton shook his head. "It's the last thing I can do for Sue Ellen. I'll build her burial box," he whispered. "And welcome somethin' to do. . . ."

Fanny nodded. "Work's one answer to grief, Alton. You've your work laid out for you in raisin' up three motherless young'uns. But you can count on me an' my Lizzie to help you out. And don't go protestin', my man. With the two new babes, you're goin' to have to accept helpin' hands."

"I'm in your debt," Alton acknowledged, realizing even in his grief that Fanny's practical nature would not let him linger there long.

"I have Sue Ellen laid out on the cooling board," Fanny broached the painful subject. "When you have her coffin built—I'll dress her in her buryin' gown and help you prepare her for the neighbors' arrival. Folks will be comin' to sit up with the family tonight."

Alton wiped his eyes. "I'd better get to buildin' that box," Alton said in a numb tone.

Fanny turned away. Alton stared after her, then, like a

sleepwalker, wandered across the lawn toward the shed where the oak lumber was stored. Consciously, he focused on the task at hand, selecting board after board of prime wood.

He'd barely set to work when he heard the bell in the church tower down the road begin the mournful tolling—one gong for each year of Sue Ellen's earthly life.

The boards piled before him were wet when he mustered the will to begin his onerous task.

By midnight the box was built.

By morning the hole was dug.

By afternoon the burial before grieving neighbors was completed.

The mourners moved away to partake of the meal the neighborhood women had brought in. Laughter and teasing were absent from Lizzie's lips as she and Harmon Childers escorted Jeremiah from his mother's gravesite.

Will lingered behind.

"Need any help, Al?" he asked softly as Alton leaned heavily on the shovel.

"No . . . thanks," Alton whispered. "Just leave me alone . . . alone with Sue Ellen. . . . Please."

With each thud of earth, Alton's heart echoed dully. Steadily he worked. Finally the job was done.

Although he lived, Alton felt dead.

Hot tears coursed down his cheeks. He stared at the mound of sod embracing his Sue Ellen. His face crumpled. Unmindful of the wetness or the sticky mud, Alton threw himself across her cold grave.

"I cain't never love again, Sue! Why did you make me promise?!" he sobbed over and over. "Cain't never . . . *never!*"

Eventually Alton lifted himself from the hard ground, shivering inside his filthy clothes. He turned toward the cabin.

Never, never, never, never—his footsteps seemed to echo.

Alton wished that he had not given his vow. Love had brought him great joy. Now love had brought him even greater grief. So great that he could not bear the thought of that kind of pain again.

Never.

But you promised me. . . . A sighing reminder was carried on the gentle wind.

You gave me your word.

II
Lizzie

chapter
8

DAYS, THEN WEEKS, passed in a numb, unending blur for Alton as he struggled to adapt himself to being both pa and ma to Jem, Katie, and the two babies, Marissa and Molly.

He was grateful for Fanny and Lizzie's pleasant, cheerful participation in running the household until Lizzie became so great with her coming child that she remained on the Childers' homestead and Fanny's visits became more and more infrequent.

A thousand times a day, it seemed, Alton found himself turning from his work, intent on sharing a word with Sue Ellen. A thousand times a day his heart broke anew when he looked up, found her absent, and realized all over again that she was gone.

Jeremiah was silent in his grief. Alton knew that Jem's suffering and loss were great, and he gave the young man his privacy to work through his mourning in his own way.

After Fanny began to stop in every other day, then slacked to every third day, finally contenting herself with a random check once a week, Jem pitched in. Between the two of them, Alton believed, they performed satisfactorily to provide for the motherless little girls.

One mild winter evening not long after Harmon and Lizzie had become parents of another son, Jeremiah retreated to the attic after supper. A short time later, he reappeared, slicked up, obviously ready to depart.

"Goin' out?" Alton asked, unable to hide his surprise.

"If you don't mind," Jeremiah said, not meeting his eyes. "And if you have no objection to my use of the team."

"Be good for you to get out an' about, Jem," Alton assured. "And the team's yours for the takin'. You handle Doc and Dan as well as I do. But be mindful of icy spots on the trail."

Jem nodded. "I'll be careful."

"Uh, goin' to visit Harm an' Lizzie and see their new young'un?" Alton asked.

"Nossir. Not tonight."

"Oh, then I 'spose you'll be sparkin' the Nash girl then." Alton's comment was more a statement of fact than a question. Jem's flinch went unnoticed.

"Reckon not," he murmured in a morose tone.

"Thought you was sweet on her!" Alton said.

Jem was a long time answering. "Reckon I was."

Alton dried his large hands, softened by dishwater, on one of Sue Ellen's daintily embroidered cotton towels.

"You two have a fallin' out, son?" he inquired gently after pouring the basin of water into the slop jar.

Jem avoided his eyes. "Carrie Nash got married the other week, Pa. I thought you heard Lizzie Childers teasing me about it. Ragging me about losing my girl to a traveling man who beat my time."

Alton stared, dazed. Sudden realization washed over him. He'd been bobbing along on the surface of life, caught up in the day-to-day activities demanded of a man newly widowed and left with small children, while his son was drowning in misery.

"Guess I didn't pay no mind to Lizzie's joshin', Jem. Seems to me, though, 'tain't no jokin' matter when a feller loses his best gal to another."

Alton's sympathy was the last straw. Jem's eyes brimmed with tears of loss, then of rage.

"Pa, you can't lose something 'til you've gained it!" he flared. "I never had a chance after Ma died. Thanks to the twins—I was found courtin' too slow!"

It was the first indication that Alton had of Jeremiah's quiet, smoldering resentment. Stunned, Alton stared at the boy. How blind he'd been since Sue Ellen's passing, seeing only his own heartache and the unending work he must do to keep the family going. Now, it was as if a veil had been lifted from his eyes, and he was witnessing raw fury, unsettling in his once mild-mannered son.

"Jem, I'm sorry, son . . . so sorry."

Sorry that he hadn't seen more to the young man's needs. Sorry that he hadn't sacrificed more himself. Sorrier yet that Jeremiah seemed to blame the tiny babes, who thrived and bloomed beneath the clumsy masculine care provided them. Sorry that Jem had lost his girl, Carrie. Sorry, too, that in his grief the boy had sought to lay blame rather than to face the painful fact, set his disappointment aside, and accept it as the will and purpose of God as Alton had managed to do with the loss of his beloved wife.

"Jem . . ." Alton picked through his meager vocabulary for the right words to frame his thoughts.

Alton wanted to tell Jem of enduring, abiding love. Explain the will of God. Impart understanding regarding the seasons of life. And so much more. Alton wanted to remind the boy of his faith and to keep his promise to Sue Ellen that he would nourish her children's belief in the ways of the Lord.

But Jem would have none of it. His face was uncharacteristically hard, his eyes steely as he turned away, fleeing the situation he found a personal torment.

"I'll be going, Pa . . . *Alton* . . . ," Jem muttered, and he erupted from the cabin, banging the door behind him.

Alton was struck speechless. Drop-mouthed, he stared after Jeremiah, helpless to call him back, reeling from the shock of the boy's angry rejection. He recalled well the warmth that had filled him the first time Jem had hesitantly called him "Pa." Now Alton felt the full force of another kind of loss— this young man, Sue Ellen's son, as dear to him as his own blood daughters.

In that moment of defiance, Jeremiah had clearly drawn the battle lines. Alton was no longer "Pa." They were antagonist and adversary.

Alton stayed up through the long hours of the night.

Even after the little girls had long since fallen into slumber, he waited. Finally he fell asleep in the rocking chair near the hearth. He roused only when Jem returned home in the wee hours of the morning, the reek of whiskey and cheap perfume clinging to his clothing. Alton said nothing, and, after helping the boy to his rafter room, he stumbled into his own bed, lying awake until dawn broke.

Jem was sullen the following morning. He spoke little to Alton, although no mention was made of the previous night. Instead, Alton unburdened to Fanny Preston when she stopped by that afternoon to look in on the little girls.

"'Tis difficult for Jeremiah," she said. "A more comely gal than Carrie Nash is hard to find," she sighed, resigned. "But pretty is as pretty does. I, for one, give praise to God that Carrie ran off with another, no doubt a bloke of like mind, before causin' our Jeremiah grief. He'd not have rested content, yoked with someone like Carrie, who don't know and love the Lord."

Alton nodded. "I gave some thought to that, too, when he began courtin' her. But I didn't 'low as how he'd be gettin' serious about the gal. Guess I didn't hear Lizzie's teasin' Jem 'bout him courtin' too slow, neither."

"Oh, that Lizzie!" Fanny said, exasperated. "You know how that girl is—impulsive as a kitten—not measurin' her words, sometimes speakin' too soon, other times not soon enough."

"I know," Alton said. "Jem feels stung by her remarks. But I know she meant no harm."

Fanny went on. "Lizzie an' Harm have always had a soft spot in their hearts for Jeremiah. Love him like family, they do! I'll wager she thought teasin' Jem was about like banterin' with our Rory!"

Alton nodded, but his brow was furrowed in a frown. "I'm right worried about Jem, Fanny, afraid he'll turn from the Lord. And I gave my word to Sue Ellen—"

"Do the best you can, Alton, and leave the rest to the Lord," Fanny cautioned. "Lecture Jem and you'll only harden his heart. Sue Ellen—an' you—raised him right. It'll stick with him and he'll return to the ways of God." She fell silent a moment. "But I know it can be pure misery to watch a loved one detour from the path of righteousness."

With Fanny's words comforting his heart and Scripture at his fingertips as he fumbled through the pages of Sue Ellen's Bible, Alton spent the long nights, rocking one baby or another and waiting for Jeremiah to come home from his drinking and carousing. Throughout, Alton held his tongue.

Months passed. Eventually there was no restraining the words that sizzled in his mind, then burned a scorching path to his lips.

"Your Mama must be turnin' in her grave, Jeremiah Stone, maybe even ruin' the day she and your pa named you after a great prophet! She didn't raise you to spend your money on trollops and travesty! Iffen you weren't a man in your own right, I'd thrash you like a spoiled, spiteful child. An' mark my words—I ain't promisin' I won't someday become righteously riled an' do it anyway. What's got into you, boy?"

"I don't want to talk about it," Jem said in an indifferent tone. He turned to leave.

Roughly Alton spun him around, forcing the boy to stare up into his glowering face.

"Mebbe I do!" Alton bellowed. "You can hate me for all you're worth! Blame me for your mama's death! Shy away from two wee, innocent babes you find guilty along with me for robbin' you of your ma. But the fact remains, Jeremiah, that I love you! Couldn't love you more if I was your natural pa. Your ma knew of my love for you and she asked me to promise her that I'd raise her children up in the faith of Christ, and I agreed, Jeremiah! Alton Wheeler keeps a promise, and won't be goin' back on his word to a dyin' woman!" he thundered. "Even if it means I have to cuff an upstart pup to get his attention an' set him back on the right path!"

Alton expected a sarcastic response. Maybe even a scuffle if Jem lunged to accost him, but he was not prepared for the younger man's retreat. Jem doubled over in grief, staggering toward the ladder leading to the attic, where he could seek solace and escape Alton's wrath.

Alton crossed the room, pulled Jem from the bottom rung, forcing the smaller man to face him—a prodigal son. Alton drew Jem into his arms.

"I'm sorry, Pa . . . I'm sorry . . . ," Jem cried quietly, then with the harsh gulping sound of a bewildered, penitent child.

Alton's heart soared. *Pa!* Jem had called him Pa!

"I know you're hurtin', son. Know you've grieved like the

rest of us over your ma, and now Carrie. But why—why did you trouble me so? Why were you ornery as cat droppin's when I had so much else fillin' my mind? Why? I'd just like to know."

Jeremiah shrank from Alton, and the older man released him. Jem presented his back to him.

"In hopes you'd tire of the treatment and run me off, Pa. So I could find a life of my own without the guilt of deserting you and the girls."

"But *this* is your life," Alton started to say. Suddenly realizing that it was not true, he bit off the words.

"Why didn't you come to me and tell me of your feelin's 'stead of schemin' that way? We could have settled things peaceable between us, 'cause that's the way your ma would've wanted it." Alton shook his head sorrowfully. Then he turned to confront his son. "You can have your rightful inheritance, Jem. I'll help you build a cabin, an' give you use of the team any time you want . . . Then I'll help you buy a couple good mules. . . ."

Jem's eyes lit up. The offer of freedom . . . a place of his own! He turned the idea over in his mind, relishing the thought. Then, manfully, he straightened his shoulders, standing nearly as tall as Alton.

"Thanks, Pa. But no. I'll stay on and help you with my little sisters. That's my place—for now. And when it comes time for me to build a life apart from you and the girls, Pa . . . as God is my witness, you'll be the first to know."

Alton nodded, too full for words. When he had composed himself, he found there were yet things that needed to be said.

"Jem, 'bout Carrie Nash. I'm sorry. Truly sorry that your heart was broke."

Jem gave him a long look. "I'm not," he admitted. "Leastways, not any more. I understand better about love,

125

now. Flighty girls like Carrie—and some others I've met—," he flushed and ducked his head for a moment, "can leave a man satisfied, yet still hungry. Do you know what I'm saying, Pa? There's a girl for me, Pa, somewhere—a good girl," Jem said, staring off into the distance before facing Alton with a clear gaze. "We'll recognize each other in God's own time. Ma told me that about you and her. And I know in my heart it will be the same for me."

Alton asked no questions, but squeezed Jem's shoulder. "Your mama'd be proud to hear you speak those words, son—as proud as I am. An'," Alton turned away, "I'll be prayin' for that gal who'll someday be so special to you . . . to all of us. . . ."

Alton and Jeremiah faced the coming spring united in their care of the little girls who thrived beneath their well-intentioned if sometimes clumsy ministrations.

The blithe months of spring gave way to scorching summer. Idle moments were rare. If there were not weeds to hoe from the garden, water to carry to tiny plants, fields to tend, and berries to pick and dry or simmer into sweet jams, there were endless vats of laundry to boil, scrub, and hang on the line strung between trees, with baby clothes laid on the grass to bleach beneath the sun.

Fanny and Lizzie helped out as they could, generously caring for the babies in their homes to free Alton and Jem to work in the fields.

"Our thanks will have to do," Alton murmured to Lizzie and Fanny time and again when he collected the little girls, "until you're better paid," he added, although he knew that neither Fanchon nor Lizzie considered him in their debt.

Fall arrived. With the chillier weather Jem and Alton entrusted the care of the girls more and more to Fanny and

Lizzie. The men would have to redouble their efforts to get the timber cut and hauled by the wagonload before bad weather set in for good.

"Best be leavin' Katie, Marissa, an' Molly with me from now on, Alton," Fanchon suggested one cold November day. "Lizzie's in the family way again. I don't mind keepin' the young'uns, an' plan on keepin' Lizzie's youngsters, too, so's she can get a mite more rest. Be needin' it, she will, presentin' us with another grandbaby come spring."

"We've almost got the full supply of wood we'll be needin' for the winter, Fanny," Alton said. "We 'preciate what you womenfolk have done for us. The day may come when we can return the favor. Mebbe I can help Will for a day or two. I've noticed his rheumatiz is troublin' him."

"That'd be right nice. He'd enjoy your company, Al, as much as he'd welcome a helpin' hand. He's missed you a powerful lot since you've been so busy with the little'uns."

"I've missed Will, too," Alton said. "The last few times I've happened by, he and Rory were over at Harm's, helpin' out."

"That Harm's a worker," Fanny said approvingly. "Thank God for that—with them facin' another mouth to feed. Harm's sort of hankerin' to build on to their cabin so's they'll have more room. They'll be haulin' out timber soon."

"Then tell him to holler when he needs an extry pair of hands," Alton reminded her, loading Katie and the two babies into the wagon.

Just as they were about to begin the journey home, sharp cries drew their attention to the trail.

"That's Will, Rory, Lizzie, and all of her kids," Fanny said. "Wonder what the ruckus is about?"

Even from that distance they could see that Lizzie had cushioned herself on the wagon bed, pillowing Harmon's prostrate form in her arms as the terrified children spilled around her. Will was driving the team, with Rory braced against the wagon seat—his posture strangely stiff.

"Oh dear God, no! There's been an accident!" Alton cried.

Fanchon clutched up her hem and pittered down the frozen path as quickly as her plump feet would carry her. When Lizzie looked up and saw her, she bawled brokenly.

"*Mama!* Mama, do somethin', Harmon's hurt bad! You'll know what to do! Help him!" The pleading in her voice was that of a small child begging her mother to mend a rag doll or soothe a hurt with a kiss and a pat.

But Alton, only a step behind Fanny, saw her recoil at the sight of Harmon Childers looking more dead than alive.

Lizzie moved aside. Fanchon loosened Harm's shirt. When she unfastened the buttons, gore spilled out, and she hastily closed the opening, blanching in remembrance of the bright red blood and the shiny, curling parts unfamiliar to her past healing experiences.

"Harm needs a doctor," Fanny said.

Will's voice was gentle. "Harm's beyond doctorin'. We can only commit him to the Lord. See to Rory's needs, Mama."

Only then did Fanny look away from the horror that was Harmon's crushed form to regard her son. His trousers were slashed to the thigh—his leg twisted at a peculiar angle. Blood had darkened the material. She gingerly pushed the flapping cloth away from the wound, then gasped to see bone and marrow protruding from the torn flesh.

"Drive on to the doctor's, Will," Fanchon said, boosting herself up into the wagon. "Rory's goin' to lose that leg. I've borne a lot in all o' my years, but I can't bear to rend the limb from a child I brought into this world. I just can't do it. . . ."

She looked into Rory's stricken face and realized what her honesty had cost him.

"An' besides—mayhap the doctor can work a miracle—

128

iffen we get there fast enough," she quickly added, but there was little hope in her heart or in Rory's pain-glazed eyes.

Taking command, Alton transferred Lizzie's little ones to his shoulders and promised to keep them in his care until Fanny's return.

"Hurry, Will! An' you, Lizzie! Calm yourself, gal! Think of what you're doin' to Harm's baby. 'Stead o' sobbin' and blubberin' at me to do somethin', turn your spirit toward the Lord so's poor Harmon can have some peace."

Instantly Lizzie was shaken from her hysteria. She clutched Harmon's hand until her knuckles were white, but he made no move to complain.

Alton looked at him and felt a hollowness within. Harmon Childers was beyond feeling fresh pain. Alton knew that before Will could drive the team half a league, Lizzie's husband would reach a place of everlasting peace.

Alton comforted the children and tucked them into the wagon with vain assurances. Helplessly he stared after Will's buckboard as it proceeded down the road, bearing the wounded men. *Thank the Lord the creeks weren't out,* Alton thought as he watched their departure. Suddenly there was a penetrating wail that pierced the crystalline afternoon air. In that moment, as the sun began to sink toward the west, Alton knew Lizzie Childers had become a widow.

En route home Alton stopped at the small church. He grasped the cold rough rope affixed to the cast-iron bell, giving it a jerk, and the first peal rang out over the hilly countryside. Carefully he counted twenty-two clanging gongs to inform those, who stopped to count, the identity of the one who had gone on.

A half-hour later the team leaned into the harness and hauled the wagon onto the lane leading up to the cabin, where Jem had the evening meal waiting. Expecting Alton and the girls, he was startled to find the Childers' family in tow.

"I'll explain, private-like," Alton said, giving Jem an expression that bade him ask no more questions. "Dish up plates for the young'uns. We can rustle up somethin' to eat when we've tended to their needs."

Kate, Molly, and Marissa saw no cause for excitement, and Lizzie's children, with no comprehension of the awful reality that had befallen them, ate heartily, laughing and giggling at the novelty of eating together in the Wheeler cabin.

After the youngsters were scrubbed and placed before the hearth for quiet play, Jem and Alton neatened up as best they could and Alton explained the events as they had unfolded.

"Lizzie's in the family way again," he said. "Fanchon confided in me today. Harm, Will, an' Rory have been loggin' firewood, and timberin' for some lumber to build onto their place. The accident must've happened in the woods. I didn't get no partic'lars. But I could tell Harm was done for, and now those little'uns and the new'un on the way don't have no pa." He lowered his voice, glancing into the front room, where the smaller children, rosy-cheeked from the fire, were growing drowsy.

It was later, when a neighbor dropped in, that they learned all the details of the afternoon.

"Harm and Rory was usin' a two-man crosscut, workin' to fell a big oak," he began, then went on to explain that the massive tree had shifted, settled squarely, and pinched the saw blade so it wouldn't move a hairsbreadth. "They tried choppin' with axes, but it didn't do no good, so they chained up Will's horses to the tree. Thought they could jerk it off the stump." The neighbor paused, pondering how to tell the rest. "The horses moved too fast, and that tree fell where they was least expectin' it to. Landed smack across Harmon an' got

Rory's leg—you could hear it snap like kindlin', Will said. If it hadn't been for the leaf cover in the woods to cushion him, Harm wouldn't have lasted as long as he did."

"Poor Lizzie," Jem murmured, when they were alone again, the Childers' children sleeping on pallets near the hearth, their own little ones tucked safely into bed.

Alton nodded. "Don't know how that poor girl's goin' to get by," Alton said. "Will's gettin' too old and crippled up to help much. Rory, with a leg missin', will be laid up for quite some time. With her husband gone and the young'uns to raise—" Alton shook his head over Lizzie's dire straits. "And another one on the way."

"She'll get by," Jem said. "Lizzie's tough as rawhide. The Lord will see her through . . . and," he added softly, "I plan to do all in my power to help."

"Guess they'll be needin' all the help they can get," Alton sighed.

Jem was silent for a long while. "Mind if I take the team tonight, Pa?"

Alton gave him a worried glance. Surely he wasn't going to town—to retreat into the loose life he had lived after Sue Ellen's death. But when Alton encountered the tall stance of his son and noticed the way his shoulders seemed to have visibly broadened, Alton felt shamed for his moment of suspicion.

"What I have is yours, son. You know that," Alton said.

"I'll be going over to Lizzie and Harm's, then, to feed their stock. I'll do the same at Will and Fanny's."

"They'll 'preciate it, Jem," Alton murmured, himself touched by the generous gesture.

"I may wait around a bit, if you don't need me to come right home," Jem said. "In case there's news—"

"I'd considered suggestin' it."

Jem returned hours later. Children were asleep on make-shift pallets as every quilt Sue Ellen owned was spread on the hard wood floor. Alton kept the fire stoked, and the cabin radiated warmth and welcome.

"Reckon we'd best plan on keeping Lizzie's young'uns for a few days, anyway, Pa. Harm's dead—just as you figured. Rory's leg had to come off at the knee. Doc's keeping Rory overnight, just to make sure the bleeding doesn't start up again. When he saw the state Lizzie was in, he allowed as how he'd better keep Lizzie a day or two, as well."

"We'll keep the children," Alton said. "Will and Fanny will have enough to do, tendin' to the buryin' plans, and preparin' for Rory and Lizzie to come home."

But infection set into Rory's wound. The doctor kept him in his care long after he released Lizzie, just in time for her to return to the Salt Creek community to witness Harm's burial in the walnut coffin Will had on hand.

Days later Will was building an oak coffin to be stored in the space just vacated. "Best keep one handy," he explained to Alton. "Each time I make a burial box, I always think this one could be my own. One of these days . . . it will be."

"Now, Will—," Alton protested.

Will seemed unmindful of his presence. "Generally, I ain't one to question the ways an' wisdom o' the Lord, but why couldn't He have took an ol' codger like me, 'stead of a young man in his prime—like Harm?"

Alton had no answer.

Brusquely Will measured a board, sawed it neatly, and found the fit to be exact. With a soft puff he blew away a powdering of sawdust, then reached for a screwdriver.

"Why? Oh, why?" he sighed his sad question again.

chapter
9

CHRISTMAS WAS a joyous respite from the long season of despair wrought by Sue Ellen's passing and Harm's violent death.

Insisting that they all needed a change from their grinding routines, Fanny planned a Christmas feast.

While Jeremiah tended Katie and the twins, Alton traveled on horseback to Watson and picked through the supply of fancies in the small general store to find Christmas surprises for his little girls. For Lizzie and Fanny, he purchased yard goods. For Will, a shaving brush. For Jeremiah, a new shirt and trousers.

Alton and Jeremiah clumsily attempted to decorate the cabin that was woefully barren of a woman's touch. After telling his babes the story of the Virgin Birth, marked for him in a Bible Tom McPherson had given him one lonely Christmas in the coal camp, Alton drew out his harmonica and began to play. But without Sue Ellen's sweet voice, the rendition was mournful and bleak, the experience more painful than pleasant, and Alton put his instrument away.

Christmas Day dawned clear and bright.

Alton's breath froze in the air as he harnessed the team and

133

prepared to travel to Fanny and Will's farm. Sunlight sparkled like fiery gems sprinkled over the fields and pastures.

Bundling the children until they could scarcely move, Alton and Jeremiah carried Katie and the twins to the wagon, then swaddled them in a crackling nest of golden straw.

A short while later they arrived at the Preston farm and were met by Fanchon, who exhibited more cheer than she had since the accident that claimed Harm's life and cost Rory his leg. Will was in her wake and even Rory hobbled forth to welcome the visitors to their Christmas table.

"Alton, would you do us a favor and go fetch Lizzie an' her young'uns?" Fanny asked. "'Twould save Will hitchin' up our team."

"Be glad to do it," Alton said.

"I'll go, Pa," Jeremiah said quickly, and Alton gave him an assessing glance, but did not question him.

"Generous of you, son," Alton murmured. He swung down from the wagon, hauling his little girls into his arms. "I'll be cozy by the fire while you're shiverin' in the wind."

"I don't mind," Jem retorted. "I can do some of the chores while Lizzie's readying the little ones. It'll save me time this evening."

"Don't dawdle too long, Jeremiah!" Fanny reminded. "I'm about to add thickenin' to the meat drippin's for gravy!"

Jem nodded and clucked to the team.

Alton watched him go, then ducked his tall frame through the door of the homey Preston cabin to warm his hands by their blazing fire.

"They're here!" Fanny announced, hearing the snort of the great Clydesdales. She left the cabin, with Alton a step behind.

"Merry Christmas, Granny!" Lizzie's children called.

134

"Merry Christmas, darlin's!" Fanny replied, laughing as she folded Thad and Lester into her arms, giving Alton charge of Maylon.

Jem had already swung down from the wagon and circled around to help Lizzie from the high seat. His overly solicitous manner was not lost on Alton, nor was the way in which the young man eased Lizzie's weight onto himself to lighten the load she bore. Neither did it escape Alton's attention that, as Jem's hands spanned Lizzie's swollen waist with her face only inches from his, she smiled—for the first time since Harm's death—and her eyes warmed with the glint of suppressed laughter.

After safely tucking Lizzie Childers into a chair drawn near the hearth, Jem remanded her into her mother's care, then turned his attention to the needs of the team.

With Lizzie looking on, feeling guilty for "bein' so lazy-like," Fanny dished up steaming bowls of mashed potatoes, gravy, yams, corn, and sliced ham, followed by small jars of condiments and preserves. With a rustle of activity, the group found places around the long table, made festive by Fanny's best dishes and a centerpiece of holly, bright with berries.

The aromas floated up to envelop them, tempting the little ones to try "just a bite." But Fanny, wiping a skim of moisture from her brow, put out a restraining hand.

"Not until after the blessin'," she frowned. "Will, do you mind if Jem offers our thanks?"

"'Twas goin' to request it myself," conceded Will.

Jem cleared his throat, bowed his head, and thanked the Lord for the many blessings bestowed on them—peace in their pain, hope for the future, and for the precious gift of the Birthday Babe born so long ago that they might have a Savior and Comforter in times of trial.

"In His precious name we pray, amen," Jem finished his eloquent prayer.

Quickly Alton took a peek at Lizzie. As she lifted her head, her eyes sought Jem's and, for an instant, she was radiant with admiration, her pretty face aglow.

Alton reckoned that the knowledge of Jem's and Lizzie's budding attraction to one another was scarcely hidden from the others. Fanny and Will treated Jem as a favored son; Rory, with the camaraderie of a brother. Lizzie teased Jem— as she always had from the first moment of their meeting— but now it was not the amusement of a married woman for a youth less than five years younger but the fond banter of equals.

The simple gifts were exchanged, Lizzie and Fanny exclaiming over the pretty fabric that would be made up into new spring dresses, the children still hugging cornhusk dolls received earlier in the day and whistles whittled from hickory wood.

Fanny popped corn over the fire and served creamy chocolate fudge, rich with hickory nuts harvested in the autumn months. They drank of apple cider, sparkling cold, aged to a ripe tang.

"We'd best be headin' home soon, son," Alton said, drowsy with contentment, "or I'm liable to take root right here in this chair."

Jeremiah glanced toward Lizzie. "Would you like me to take you home, Liz, so your pa won't have to take his team out today?"

Lizzie nodded. "That's right thoughtful, Jem." She raised her voice. "Children, get your wraps on! Uncle Jem's goin' to take us home. Lester! You dress warm—you can help with the chorin' when we get there."

The children moved into action. Jem helped them with

buttons. Lizzie collected their presents and tucked them away in her canvas satchel. She embraced her mother, then drew on her heavy wrap.

"Merry Christmas, Mama," she whispered before her voice cracked and her eyes misted with tears.

Fanny gave her a hard hug. "None of that, now. There'll be many more Merry Christmases for you, honey. The Lord will provide."

Biting her lip, Lizzie herded her children toward the door. Alton drifted behind her. Jem lifted the children into the wagon and laughingly ducked a snowball that Lester had concealed to pitch at him. Lizzie clucked with concern, but Jem halted her reprimand. A little funning would do the children no harm, he was thinking with a new kind of concern.

As Alton was about to close the door behind them, he noticed Jem settling Lizzie into the buckboard. From beneath his coat, Jem produced a small, awkwardly wrapped package that he pressed into Lizzie's hands.

Held captive by his own curiosity, Alton looked on through the slitted door.

"For you, Liz," Jeremiah said softly. "I figured you—being a widow and all—wouldn't have a present to open this year . . . from a . . . man who loves you—"

"Oh, Jem—," Lizzie breathed.

And the loving smile she cast at him was the greatest gift of all, one Alton knew that Jem would produce time and again from the stored treasures of his heart to be examined with joy, not only on Christmas but every day of their lives.

By the time Jeremiah returned from Lizzie's farm, Alton had the little girls ready to make the trip to their own cabin and enough leftovers, supplied by Fanny, to last the rest of the week.

Back home Jem did the choring while Alton fired the embers in the hearth to create a roaring blaze that quickly heated the small room. The children were showing signs of weariness. Jem and Alton served them their supper, then scrubbed them with warm, soapy water, brushed their hair, dressed them in woolly flannel gowns, and tucked them into bed.

The two men seated themselves before the fire. No words passed between them for some time, while their own private thoughts whirled.

"Pa—" Jeremiah's whisper broke the stillness.

Alton roused from his musings. "Yes?"

"I've something I want to ask you—get your advice on what I should do."

"I'll do my best, son," he nodded solemnly. "I've always tried to give you wise counsel, though I'm just a man, the Lord knows."

Jem nervously licked his lips. "It's about Liz—Lizzie Childers." He halted as the words crowded his brain until he didn't know which to choose first.

"Go on," Alton urged.

"Well, I was thinking . . . you'd know best what I am suffering, Pa, being as you went through it with Ma . . . and her a widow woman at the time."

"Just what was you thinkin', son?" Alton's pulse quickened, knowing already what Jem's answer would be.

"Do you think folks would talk if I were to make Liz my wife? So soon after Harm's passing, I mean?"

"I don't know, son," Alton replied truthfully. "Have you talked this over with Lizzie?"

Brusquely Jeremiah shook his head. "Didn't want to chance offending her—the way I feel about her. And wanted to have your idea if she'd accept me or not."

138

Alton nodded. "I saw the way Lizzie looked at you, son. I don't doubt she'll have you. But she might need time—her grief's still fresh."

"I've loved Lizzie Childers for as long as I can remember," Jeremiah admitted boldly, "though I didn't know it at the time. She's always amused me, made me laugh, feel good. I never know what she'll do next. And I want to protect her and make her smile the way she used to. And, Pa," Jem said, looking straight into Alton's eyes, "I want to take care of her children the way you took care of me."

Alton cleared his throat. "Sure 'nuff sounds like love to me. That's how I felt about your mama—an' you."

Jem stared, unseeing, into the fire, his expression suddenly grave. "But Ma turned you down, Pa! And she was a widow longer than Liz. I'm hankering to ask Lizzie to wed, but—," he shook his head in confusion, "if I did, Liz might not think it seemly. She might feel the neighbors would be scandalized. I don't think she could bear being the target of gossip—not after what she's been through."

"I don't think folks around here are the gossipin' kind," Alton said, spreading his hands. "They didn't talk when Oscar Blye over t' Watson remarried, with his wife in the ground scarce a month, an' him with a houseful o' little ones. An' they didn't talk much when Widow Hodson joined up with that new feller only a wee while after her man got killed tryin' to break that maverick horse."

"That's true," Jem agreed. "She had crops in the field needing to be harvested and children to feed—just like Lizzie."

"In my heart, Jem, I don't think folks'd judge Lizzie hard—nor you."

"That's what I'm hoping," Jem sighed, voicing his plans. "I've tried to think how I would feel if I was Harm . . . and,

Pa, I can't help but believe Harmon would approve. That he'd be happy to know Liz and his young'uns were being cared for by someone who loves them."

"I think you're right. Harm knew you were his friend. I think he'd be pleased to have you protectin' his kin, pleased to know you love his Lizzie."

"It's settled then," Jeremiah said. "I'm going to ask her. Not the next chance I get, though. Think I'll hold off 'til New Year's. Sort of like heralding a fresh time of happiness after a long year of trials and trouble."

After that Alton noticed that Jeremiah tarried in the evenings when he visited Lizzie's farm to tend to the chores.

On New Year's Day, Fanny invited them again to partake of a holiday meal. This time Jeremiah took the reins, and, as Alton and the girls entered the cabin to celebrate with Will and Fanny, Jeremiah continued on to fetch Lizzie and her brood.

With Jem having confided in him, Alton watched the young couple with new interest, noting a sense of unity growing between them. When the afternoon grew late, Jem took Lizzie home so she could get her rest, then did the chores before returning to collect Alton and the little ones.

Alton gave him a helplessly inquiring gaze. Jem grinned broadly, unable to contain his happiness.

"She said yes, Pa! Just like you reckoned she would!" Jem said.

"Congratulations, son. You're gettin' a fine girl," Alton murmured.

Suddenly, though he was surrounded by three small girls tugging on his trouser legs, Alton felt an aching, hollow loneliness inside.

"It won't be for a while," Jem said, so absorbed in his own

140

happiness that he failed to see the anguish on his father's face. "When I asked Liz to wed, she said yes but allowed as to how it'd be for the best if we wait 'til after the babe comes."

Alton nodded. "Sound judgment on Lizzie's part."

"But I'll still go over and lend a hand and see her when I want. Knowing that she's agreed to be mine makes the waiting more tolerable."

"The time will pass quickly," Alton predicted.

Jem agreed. "There's so much to do—both at our place—and at hers."

"I'll help in any way I can," Alton promised. "You know that."

"I was counting on it, Pa."

"Goin' to miss you, Jem," Alton said, striving for a casual tone, even though the words clutched in his throat. "Won't be the same around here, 'thout you."

Jeremiah gave a stiff nod. "A feeling returned—though I know Liz—and I'll wager you'll see about as much of us and the children as if we lived with you. And you and the girls will be welcome any time."

Quietly the young couple's betrothal was announced to family members and close friends who awaited the birth of Lizzie's baby with increased interest, knowing that not long afterward a wedding would take place.

Winter conceded to the demands of an early spring, and when March arrived like a lamb, Lizzie's baby—a girlchild—was named Harmony.

Lizzie, buoyed by her newfound happiness, quickly regained her strength, and the neighbors, hungry for a reason to celebrate after the tragic winter, anticipated a festive wedding. But it was not to be.

"Liz and I have decided that, out of respect for Harm's

memory, a simple ceremony with only the family present would be more fitting," Jeremiah explained.

"Lizzie's got a sound head on her shoulders," Alton agreed.

"But folks are more than welcome to come for a wedding feast afterward," Jem smiled.

"They'll not be denied their celebration," Alton surmised. "I 'spect the womenfolk are already plannin' their pies and dainties."

Soft April breezes caressed the land when Alton's family joined with Will's to witness the union of their children.

Scarcely had their vows been exchanged and the symbolic kiss given, than the neighbors began to arrive, decked in their finery, bearing party delicacies and foodstuffs to burden the long plank table.

"I can't remember when I ever had so much fun!" Alton said.

"Probably not since your own weddin' to Sue Ellen," Will suggested.

At the mention of her name both men fell silent. With a gentle touch on Alton's shoulder, Will left discreetly.

Alton's thoughts spun back through the years. Sue Ellen's son, a mere lad of twelve when they met, had today become the head of a new family, with children gathered around him, a loving woman at his side, a blossoming babe cradled in her arms.

At that moment, Alton realized that full as his life might be, it was strangely empty. He missed a woman's touch, a woman's softness, a woman's love. He missed someone to share the good times and the bad—a woman like Sue.

The journey home seemed one of the longest of his life. Three sleepy heads bobbed beside him on the wagon seat, swaying in slumber, rocked by the movement of the wagon over the road.

Without Jem to share the duties, it took twice as long to tuck his daughters into bed. Then, sitting for a moment in Sue Ellen's rocking chair, Alton realized how much he missed the boy already. He had come to enjoy the last hour of the evening, keeping company with Jem before the fire, discussing the crops, the weather, the neighborhood news. There had grown up between them a manly camaraderie he would sorely miss.

It was right that Jem should have his own family, Alton mused. Right that he should know the love of a good woman. But just now the thought rankled, increasing the deep longings of his heart.

Sue Ellen! My own sweet Sue. How I need you this night! And he dropped his head, sobbing unashamedly for the love he had known and lost and would never know again.

chapter
10

ONE DAY DRIFTED into another and, at times, except when Alton read stories to his little girls or talked with them, using the simple terms that tots could understand, he felt as if his voice, his mind, would rust and lock up from disuse.

He was grateful when Jem and Lizzie happened by or insisted that he and the little ones join them for a Sunday meal after church. Although he had much to be thankful for, Alton couldn't help but ponder the lonely fallowness of his heart. More than once, he remembered his word given to Sue Ellen on her deathbed and foresaw it as a promise wisely extracted.

She knew that it was right for him to love again, as it was for Lizzie to find happiness with Jeremiah, but there was a difference. For Alton there was no woman—none he could bear to wed after the divine happiness that had been his with Sue Ellen.

Scarcely had the balmy spring breeze surrendered to the hot, scorching winds of summer, than area families' concerns turned to the school term come autumn.

Jem paid a visit to Alton one June evening. "Thad's needing some schooling, Pa," he said. "He has a quick mind and would do well with some instruction. I've taught him all I know, and he's eager for more."

Alton nodded. "It's right for the young'uns to be educated
. . . taught better than some of us are able. I've been givin'
thought to Mary Katharine's book-learnin', too."

"There are folks in Watson or Effingham, where we could
pay board and send Thad to school, but neither Liz nor I
want that for our son, Pa. He'd be lonely and we would worry
about his health and whether he was happy, or maybe wonder
if the folks we'd hired to care for him were providing for him
as we'd prefer."

"I've harbored such concerns of my own, with regards to
your sister's education," Alton admitted.

"Liz and I have talked with some of the neighbors in these
parts," Jem went on. "Ones with young'uns of school age—
and those, like Fanny and Will—with grand young'uns.
We've been considering the idea of our own school so our
children can stay at home where they belong."

The idea was so appealing, Alton wondered why he hadn't
come by it himself.

"That's a fine idea!" Alton said. "No reason why we
shouldn't."

"I figured you'd be agreeable," Jem said. "The plans so far
are for the men to work together to put up a log house for the
school and a smaller one for the teacher's home. We figure we
can't pay a big salary but are praying we'll find someone
who'd be content with a nice little cabin, plenty to eat, and a
bit of pay. Folks around here can't offer a sizeable amount of
cash but will be generous with food and time."

"The Lord will surely provide," Alton assured, "an' send us
a schoolmaster who'll accept our terms—somebody ready to
do well by our young'uns."

"We're counting on that," Jeremiah said. "There'll be a
meeting this Sunday after worship services."

The meeting was well attended. It appeared that the need

146

for a school in the community had long been recognized, but for lack of a proper schoolmaster the families had sent their young ones to the nearest town or tried to teach them at home. Now they were one in their insistence that Alton be among the three men selected to seek out a suitable instructor.

"Please accept," Fanny urged Alton. "Don't worry about the time it will take away from home an' the girls. I'll tend 'em—with a glad heart—any time there's a need. Please! You know what we be lookin' for in the person who guides our little'uns."

"All right," Alton gave in. "I'll do my part."

Having an active role in the construction of the school-house gave Alton new direction and purpose. The neighbors labored hard and long, content that, when the time came, there would be a schoolteacher for their children.

"I hate bein' away from home," Alton told Fanny when he learned that several candidates had applied for the new job. "But it's necessary if we're to find the right person."

"Don't trouble your head about Kate, Marissa, and Molly," Fanny said. "I'll have those wee beauties spoilt good an' proper by the time you return to claim 'em."

Alton gave a hearty laugh as he kissed and hugged the babies good-bye, then drove off to meet with the other two men who were to interview applicants for the new position.

They journeyed to Effingham, registered at the town's one hotel, and the next day, met privately with the applicants—both men and women—who presented themselves at the appointed hour.

One by one they filed in.

Alton and his friends exchanged glances.

Some who were qualified for the position were obviously unfit in temperament. Others, upon learning of the low pay, lost interest in the opening.

Only three candidates remained—a bookish young man, a stout, imposing matron, and a poorly clad but impeccably groomed young woman.

After bidding the three to remain in the anteroom, Alton and his neighbors conferred about the candidates' qualities and qualifications.

"The gent," Alton said, "strikes me as nice enough, an educated feller . . . but, frankly, a bit of a weak sister. The older boys wouldn't turn a tap botherin' to learn. They'd set their minds to playin' devilment upon him an' him too meek an' mild to take steps to correct 'em. Though, to be honest, I *had* leaned toward a man for the job."

"My exact sentiments," came a response.

"An' mine."

"By the looks of her, the older woman would not only be takin' the young'uns to task—but their parents as well," came one firm judgment.

"Puts me in mind of my old Aunt Hilda . . . never married and as snappish as a shrew," came a second.

"Well, since I'm in agreement, that leaves Miss Buckner," said Alton. "Her credentials ain't the best of the lot, but then she shows a carin' 'bout our young'uns that puts her in a favor'ble light."

"She's a plucky young woman," another committee member added his thoughts, "an' seems eager to make her way in the world."

The third representative nodded his approval. "She's admittedly a committed Christian, and I like that, along with the idea that she's not afraid of hard work."

"Mind, it'd be her first teachin' position," Alton said, "and her not long from an orphan's home, I understand. Doubtless she'd agree to less money and would settle for—even cotton to—neighborly support and friendship."

"There's one way to find out, Alton. Ask her."

Alton rose, crossed the worn rug, and reached for the knob. At the sound it created in the adjoining room, three pairs of eyes turned in unison to regard him hopefully.

At that instant Alton wished he were anywhere but in his own shoes, wished he could offer the lot of them gainful employment. He saw the defeat in the young man's expression and the stoic resignation in the matron's. But when he called for Miss Buckner, the apprehension in her eyes was replaced with unbounded hope and happiness.

She entered the inner room and faced the committee, nodding gently as they laid out their plans.

"I'll consider it an honor to be your schoolmarm," she said softly, "and be grateful for whatever you can offer. Already, I know that you come of generous people."

"That we do, Miss Buckner," Alton affirmed. "With your agreement, then, I guess we can make it official. You're hired!"

Miss Buckner seemed ready to swoon with relief. "Oh, thank you! I promise you—you won't regret your decision. I'll teach your little ones the best I know how—and love them like my very own."

Alton left the room to thank the remaining applicants for their time and trouble. He returned to find the committee members discussing the immediate future with Miss Abigail Buckner.

"How soon would you be able to fill the position?" they inquired of the youthful, golden-haired schoolmarm.

She flushed slightly. "As you're aware, I have no family . . . and nowhere to tarry. I'm free to begin immediately." She avoided their gazes. "In fact," she added softly, "would prefer it so I could prepare for the coming term."

"The sooner, the better then, we'd say," was the enthusiastic consensus.

"We'll stow your belongin's in my wagon," Alton said. "If you're ready, we can leave right away. Come sunset, if we've no trouble along the way, you'll be in your new home."

"Home . . . ," Miss Abigail breathed. *"Home!"*

Alton gave her a searching look. He guessed he knew something about loneliness and a lot about drifting without a firm anchor, for until Sue Ellen had come into his life, he, too, had had no place to call home.

Miss Abby hugged herself impulsively and closed her eyes as if dreaming, but when she opened them, the Salt Creek representatives were still standing there. It was not a dream.

"Gentlemen, I'm ready to go home," she whispered, favoring her new employers with one of the sweetest smiles Alton had ever seen.

III
Abigail

chapter
11

"It's worked out well, just like the Lord intended when He brought Miss Abby into our midst," Jem said with enthusiasm.

"Sure has," agreed Alton as they discussed the matter over Sunday dinner following church services that morning.

"She fits into the area like a hand in a glove," Lizzie pointed out. "And, Rory Preston, she's more than a wee bit pleasin' to the eye," she cast a teasing grin in her brother's direction, "or hadn't you noticed?"

But Rory found no opportunity to reply.

"That was the first thing Pa noticed about her," Jem chimed in. "That was qualifications enough to settle *his* mind on her."

Alton gasped. "Why, you cheeky young pup!" he blustered. "I never! It boiled down to a weak sister, a stern old crow, and Miss Abigail. Her appearance had nothing to do with our choice. Leastways, not as far as *I* was concerned."

In truth, it hadn't.

Until that moment at Fanny's dinner table, Alton had given little thought to Miss Abigail's physical attributes. Briefly he let his eyelids sink shut, the better to envision her, and he realized that she was comely indeed, with a subtle fair beauty that seemed to be awaiting her own discovery.

153

By the time Alton's thoughts caught up with the conversation, thankfully it had turned from the schoolmarm to Rory's latest conquest.

"Poor Miss Abby doesn't have a chance with our Rory, anyway," Lizzie said dismally, shaking her head. "I'm afraid he's smitten by Judith Blye. Or, perhaps Melinda Nash."

"Lizzie!" protested her brother. "That's enough!"

When Rory flushed scarlet, Lizzie giggled with glee. "Aha! So Melly, it is!" she cried triumphantly. "At least she's a decent sort—more than I can say for her big sister Carrie!" she sniffed disdainfully. "Whatever happened to that girl after she ran off and got married?" Then, not waiting for an answer, she hurried on, "Well, take my advice, Rory, and don't do like Jem did and lose your gal by courtin' too slow."

"Now, Liz, aren't you glad I *did?*" Jem retorted with a good-natured grin.

"I give thanks for that every day." Lizzie winked at Jem, but there was a serious light in her eyes.

Soon the foolishness gave way to a discussion of the harvesting of crops and the school year ahead. Alton scratched his head. Katie needed new frocks for school, yet there were the crops to be harvested and chores to be done.

"Don't give it another thought, Papa Alton," Lizzie declared. "I'll buy for Katie's needs as I do for my own young'uns."

"That'd be right nice o' you. We'll settle up when you return." And with an almost audible sigh of relief, Alton lay into his second piece of apple cobbler.

The next day Jem and Lizzie borrowed Alton's team and wagon for the trip to Effingham, returning by sundown with yard goods, stockings, ink, pens, chalk, slateboards, and an array of supplies that brought whoops of delight from the children.

"You look as pretty as your mama, darlin'," Alton said, as he helped Katie dress on the first day of school. "Now you study hard, honey, and do what Miss Abigail tells you!"

Alton helped Katie into the wagon and cradled the twins, one on each knee, for the ride to the schoolhouse. And that afternoon he was back to fetch her home, encountering a radiant Miss Buckner, who was genuinely enjoying her new position and the little charges entrusted to her care.

"Mr. Wheeler! How nice to see you! I do declare—if your Mary Katharine continues to do as well as she has today, she'll go to the head of the class in no time!" And she flashed a dimple beside a ripe, rosy mouth.

Funny, Alton thought, flushing a beet-red, he'd not noticed that dimple before, nor the color of her eyes—somewhere between the blue of the cornflowers that grew beside the front stoop and the violet of a summer dusk.

Thereafter, except when the weather prevented, Katie walked the mile to and from school. For Alton, the days were long without her familiar presence, and even the little girls cried for their "Tatie." Toward evening each day, Alton found himself looking forward to the moment when she would burst through the cabin door, filling his ears with tales of the day's events and her successes in the classroom, winning smiles of approval from "Miss Abby."

"Your mama would be as proud of you as I am, Mary Katharine," he murmured, as if to counter the seemingly traitorous interest that had begun to stir each time Katie mentioned the winsome young schoolmarm.

"After you, Pa, I think Miss Abby's my favorite person in the whole, wide world."

"What about the babies?" Alton teased.

"Well, after 'Rissa and Molly," Katie changed her mind.

"Then there's Jem," Alton prompted.

Katie frowned at the reminder. "All right, after Jem and Lizzie—"

Alton suppressed a chuckle. "Reckon Fanny and Will would feel right sad to be left out."

"Oh! After Fanny, and Will, an' Rory, too!"

Alton laughed out loud, hugging the little girl to him. "I'm sure Miss Buckner would feel proud to know she has your affections, ranked right along with family, Katie."

"She already knows," Katie confessed, "'Cause I already told her. An' she says she loves me, too. Said she couldn't love me any more if she was my mama." Katie paused. "Pa . . . *could* she be my mama? Please? I could ask her tomorrow—"

Alton was shaken.

"Mary Katharine Wheeler—don't you utter one word of such nonsense to Miss Abigail! And I hope you haven't talked loosely about such things to your schoolmates. Tongues start waggin' easy enough as it is, over a widower and a marriageable woman, 'thout his own child fuelin' the fires of speculation!"

"I never said nothin', Pa," Katie said, disappointed. "I just got the idea this afternoon when I was walkin' home and thought I'd ask permission."

"I know you're wantin' a mama, sweetheart," Alton said in a soft, sad voice. "But for now, Fanny and Lizzie will have to do. I'm not ready to seek a wife."

In the future, Alton was careful not to question Katie about Miss Buckner, nor to show undue interest in the school-marm's activities.

He was cordial to Miss Abby when they met briefly among the cluster of neighbors outside the church building, but he took pains to be on his best behavior lest some careless word or gesture might provide fodder for gossiping tongues.

November arrived in a frigid blast of air, bringing an early snowfall. Although Alton was not scheduled to haul firewood to the schoolhouse for a week yet, he decided not to chance having Miss Abigail run short. He arrived early one afternoon, Doc and Dan snorting a white cloud of vapor.

"How thoughtful of you, Mister Wheeler," said Miss Abby, favoring him with one of her brightest smiles when she opened the door to admit him. Then she pressed one of the older youths into helping Alton rick up the wood near the door of her small cabin a short distance away.

That afternoon when Katie returned home, she was bubbling with news. "Miss Abby was pleased to see you today, Pa! And she'll be even happier next month!"

"Next month?"

"There's to be a Christmas program. Oh!" Katie whispered, clasping her small hands over her mouth. "It was supposed to be a s'prise. We've been practicin' some songs to sing and Miss Abby said she'd make cookies. She asked some of the older girls to help."

"I see."

"You'll be there, won't you Pa?" Katie asked.

"Of course, sugar. Marissa, Molly, and me. You couldn't keep us away with a switch!"

"Good!" Katie said. " 'Cause Miss Abby said I could be one of the angels—an' wear a white gown she's goin' to make me from a bedsheet."

"Shouldn't be hard, Katie, darlin'. You're an angel already."

Katie giggled. "That's what Miss Abby said, too, Pa!"

157

"Seems Miss Buckner's a purty smart woman."

"Just like my mama," the little girl added loyally.

Alton paused. "A whole lot like your mama."

On the night of the Christmas pageant, Alton rushed through his chores. He took extra pains with Mary Katharine and the small tots, dressing them in the frocks Lizzie and Fanny had made for them. But he had to satisfy himself with giving their tangled curls a lick and a promise before wrapping them in quilts for the drive to the schoolhouse. Mary Katharine sat beside him on the buckboard, barely able to contain her excitement.

Upon arriving, they found the building bursting at the seams with proud parents and smiling students struggling to leave an area clear for the presentation.

Miss Buckner, wearing a modest skirt and blouse, obviously her best, was bustling about, greeting her guests and tending to last-minute details. A rosy glow had taken up residence on her cheeks, and tendrils of golden hair had escaped the confinement of the tortoise-shell combs to curl fetchingly about her face.

At the appointed hour, Miss Abby blew a low, mellow note on her harmonica, and the students miraculously found their places, watching her for their cue to begin the first song. The childish voices rose as one, high and sweet, to herald the coming of the Christmas Babe. And when the parents were invited to join in, Alton found it difficult to get the words past the lump lodged firmly in his throat.

But when a small, solitary figure stepped out onto the makeshift plank platform, his heart gave a wild lurch. The cherub was garbed all in white, and affixed to her shoulders was a pair of parchment wings.

158

It was his Katie—but not the one he'd brought to the school building!

Alton's eyes grew moist with the vision before him and with the realization of his own failure as a pa. While Alton had seen to it that Katie was always clean and neat, he struggled with her buttons and bows and had given up trying to master the thick, dark, curly tresses. Tonight Miss Abby's touch had transformed his child into an angel indeed, looking so like a miniature Sue Ellen that he was breathless.

Alton applauded along with the other parents although he'd scarcely been aware of Katie's first words of announcement or of the program that followed, so deep and far-reaching were his thoughts.

Neighbors sought him out to chat over refreshments as the older school girls passed trays of sweetmeats through the audience, and Miss Buckner moved from group to group, exclaiming over the children's performance and receiving invitations to holiday dinners.

"So good to see you again, Mister Wheeler," Miss Abby greeted Alton. "Wasn't Katie wonderful?"

"An angel, she was," Alton said. "In manner—and in appearance—thanks to you."

"It was my pleasure, Mister Wheeler. I don't mind telling you—Mary Katharine is very special to me."

The twins, Molly and Marissa, one tangled around each of Alton's legs, peered out at the schoolmarm. She laughed as she saw the studied innocence in their eyes. She patted their soft, downy hair.

"I'm sure these two will be special to me when they're old enough to take their places in the classroom. That is, if the community still wants me by then."

"Don't think there's a doubt about that, Miss Buckner,"

Alton assured. "Folks are happy with the job you're doin' with our young'uns."

A shadow eased from Miss Buckner's eyes. "Well, I'm pleased to know that," she said. "I've been so happy here that the time has flown. It's hard to believe the term's half over already!" She gave Molly and Marissa another fond pat. "But I can't be sad ending one term if I have another to look forward to, now can I?"

Miss Buckner moved on.

Helplessly Alton stared after her, then abruptly jerked his gaze away so that onlookers would have no cause for speculation.

En route home, Alton was as silent as Katie was talkative. After he had readied the girls for bed, he sighed heavily and dropped into the rocker by the fire.

He reached for Sue Ellen's Bible that was resting on a small table nearby. Though he often read from the New Testament that Tom McPherson had given him, tonight he needed to feel Sue's presence as he did when he thumbed through the velvety pages that had known her touch so many times through the years.

That night as Alton skipped through the pages, reading random passages, it was as if the Lord spoke to him, delivering a message directly to his heart.

But it was not a message Alton wanted to hear.

For the Lord said: "It is not good for man to be alone."

Alton closed the Bible with a soft snap. He hardly needed to be reminded of *that!* He lived with the knowledge every day while struggling to do the best he could in fulfilling the duties of both a ma and a pa. And tonight, the transformation in his little Katie, wrought by Abigail Buckner, had been another rude reminder.

He knew he needed a helpmate, a virtuous woman, a pearl

beyond price. He knew it was not good to be alone, but he would choose that state any day over marrying someone who couldn't be to him what Sue Ellen had been!

With memories as fresh as yesterday, he compared his beloved with the women, some admittedly comely, who had crossed his path since his lonely walk from the barren ground that embraced his Sue Ellen.

None of them had found favor with him. Nor would they.

Not until Miss Abby—who was like Sue Ellen in some ways but so different in others. And if he were willing to wed her, would she even have him—him with his ignorant speech and his three little girls! With her youth and education, she could surely marry more handsomely if she chose.

Alton saw no alternative to his loneliness and contented himself that such was destined to be his lot. The women of appropriate age were already nesting, fussing over a man and a brood of young'uns like the hens in his barnyard, while the younger women of marriageable age were making bids on whippersnappers like Rory Preston—even without his leg! No, the idea of courting a woman of such tender years was pure silliness.

He considered Katie's pleas for a mama. The bitter truth was that if the twins could have known Sue's warm maternal embraces, they, too, would be raising a hue and cry to be denied a mother's love no longer.

Alton shivered against the cold emptiness of his life and the specter of a lonelier future still, when his girls were grown and had moved on to lives of their own as Jeremiah had done.

Alton decided anew that it was not good for him to be alone. He needed a helpmate—wanted a wife—but his heart rebelled against courting again. It would seem like a betrayal of all he had ever felt for Sue Ellen. The situation begged a miracle. He was a mere mortal, after all.

161

Alton's rough hands stroked the cover of the Bible as soft as Sue's skin had once been to his touch. He opened the book again, reading passage after passage. He felt his heart grow ripe, warm, and fertile with longing. A tear fell from his cheek to spot the page, blurring a word. With a soft hush the Bible slipped shut on his lap. He turned his face heavenward, then closed his eyes in anguish.

"Thy will be done," he pleaded.

With his problems given over to the Lord's care, Alton prepared for the Christmas holidays. With Lizzie's help, Katie created tasty confections in the kitchen and painstakingly crafted paper chains and scissored snowflakes to hang from threads on the cedar tree in the front room of the Wheeler cabin.

"Christmas Eve you must take supper with us," Lizzie insisted. "It wouldn't be Christmas for Jem without you and the girls, Alton—and on the morrow we'll all be at Mama's for Christmas dinner."

Jem's welcome was warm when he met Alton, lifted the girls from the wagon and swatted them through the cabin door, then stayed to help Alton with the team.

"My, but the girls are growing," Jem mused. "Especially Molly and 'Rissa. Molly's such an even-tempered, sweet child."

"That she is," Alton said.

"And 'Rissa—" Jem shook his head as words failed him to describe such stubborn willfulness in a wee tot.

"She takes after her Pa . . . in his old days," Alton said. "Molly drew from Sue, it appears, and poor 'Rissa's drawn from me."

"If so, her determination will stand her in good stead," Jem consoled.

"Or lead her down paths from which her ol' Pa can't save her. She'll need the protection of the Father Almighty himself! But, 'tis early to worry—she's only a child and at my knee, same as Molly and their older sister, listenin' to—and I pray—heedin' the Word of God."

The two men made small talk as they hitched the horses, settling feedbags over the velvety noses. Then Jem opened the cabin door and ushered Alton in.

Alton had been expecting a warm greeting from Lizzie and the shrieks of welcome from the children who flocked around him. What he had not expected was a serene, composed, carefully smiling Miss Abigail Buckner!

Alton swallowed hard.

Wordlessly his eyes sought refuge in Jem's gaze, and in his son's almost defiant stare he saw the evidence of conspiracy.

"Pa!" Lizzie called to him. "Come say hello to Miss Abby. She's agreed to dine with us. We couldn't have her alone at Christmas—not that there's any worry of that—but I asked her just ages and ages ago to bless us with her presence."

"And a blessin' it is, Miss Abby. You've as many young'uns around you as you did the night of the pageant," Alton said.

"I love children," she smiled, cuddling Molly in her lap. "Perhaps because there were always so many little ones at the orphan's home."

"It's quite obvious they love you, too," Lizzie observed.

"Speaking of the pageant," Jem added. "Your students did you proud. That performance was about the best I ever saw—except maybe for the hoedown after the barn raising for Lizzie and Harmon. That was the night Alton played his harmonica, Miss Abby. He almost created a cyclone, gasping for breath to keep the melodies spinning through the air."

Miss Abby's eyes sought Alton's. She gave him a slow

smile. "So we have something in common. In class, a harmonica is helpful when there's no piano to pitch a tune."

"I used to pass the time playin'," Alton admitted. "But I haven't made music with my harmonica in quite some time. Kind o' painful, I reckon. My wife used to like to hear me play. An' since Sue died—"

"I think I understand, Mister Wheeler," Miss Abby murmured. "But sometime I'd like to hear you play."

"Mebbe I will."

But Alton was spared from further painful recollection by the announcement that the meal was ready. With a flourish of her apron, Lizzie motioned the guests to their places.

In short order they found themselves crushed, elbow to shoulder, around the round oak table; Alton, wedged between Jeremiah on one side and Miss Buckner on the other.

The meal was a lavish display of Lizzie's culinary talents. When at last they pushed away from the table, Alton was satiated to the point of groaning. The men sat idly, enjoying the mellow mood created by the rich food and watching the children scamper around the Christmas tree.

Miss Buckner and Lizzie cleaned up in the kitchen, then joined the others around the hearth, sinking gratefully into their chairs. Still flushed from their activity, the women's faces glowed with a sheen of perspiration. Giving Miss Abby a surreptitious glance, Alton noted again that errant tendrils of hair curled moistly over her forehead and at her temples, having slipped from the confining combs. His heart gave an uncharacteristic leap, causing him to turn away abruptly, giving his attention to Jem who was beginning a recitation of the Holy Nativity.

"And it came to pass in those days, that there went out a decree from Caesar Augustus, that all the world should be taxed. . . ."

164

The familiar story, recalled from memory, nevertheless required a good bit of explanation for the small children, and Miss Abby was called upon to supply the more simple words befitting their comprehension. As she retold the tale, the firelight played upon the lovely contours of her face, and her hair gleamed golden bright. So radiant was she that, against his will, Alton was mesmerized.

". . . so it seems fitting that we sing a few Christmas carols," Jem was saying. "Besides, it'd give me an excuse to try out the fiddle Will gave me."

"Will gave you his fiddle?" Alton cried.

Jem nodded. "Said he was passing it down to the next generation, expecting me, in turn, to pass it on when the time comes."

"But . . . but . . ."

Alton's thoughts rebelled at the finality of the deed. All along Alton had chosen to ignore the signs of age besetting his good friend—the slower pace, the trembling handshake. He stared at the fiddle in his son's own strong hands. It didn't seem possible! It seems only yesterday, Alton thought, that he and Will had swayed and stomped at Harm's barn raising, breathing life into their instruments and setting the dancers' feet to flying.

It didn't seem possible that those days were gone forever, while he, Alton, marked time, living life vicariously through his daughters and Jem.

"Too bad I left my harmonica at the cabin, son," Alton said. His voice grew soft and threatened to crack with emotion. "Remember how your mama liked to hear the Christmas carols?"

"I'll never forget," Jem whispered in a strained voice. "Nor how she sang . . ."

165

They fell silent—a silence that stretched to become a living, pulsating thing.

Alton felt warm contact against his hand, then cool metal was pressed into his palm. Startled from his reverie, he saw Miss Abby retreat into the flickering shadow of the room. He stared, stupefied, at the instrument he was holding.

Dwarfed by the size of his grip was Miss Abby's harmonica, produced from her clutchbag. His eyes were drawn to hers. Nodding encouragement, she willed him to play.

Wetting his lips, Alton tested the harmonica as he might a woman's lips, found it to his liking, and formed a sweet partnership of creation.

Hesitantly Jem fingered the neck of the fiddle, scratching the bow across the catgut. The fiddle sang out a sweet chorus of notes, countering the poignant solo of the harmonica as the strains of "Silent Night, Holy Night" once again heralded the coming of Christmas.

The music of the two instruments melded, fused as one, then separated. Now it was Jem's turn to take the melody with his fiddle, sighing the sounds of a lullaby to the Christmas Babe, while Alton hummed his haunting harmony.

Suddenly, unexpectedly, from a darkened corner of the room came the clear crystal tones of a woman's voice—a voice as pure as a silver bell but resonating with the timbre of one who recognizes the joys of life because she has known its sorrows so well.

For a long, horrifying moment, Alton thought his mind was playing tricks. Every year, with the approach of the Advent season Sue Ellen had sung this song, accompanied by his harmonica. Every year, their son had listened, learning well the secret of their love, the meaning of harmony and peace on earth as God intended it when He gave His greatest gift—His only Son.

On and on it went, the sweet sighing, the merging of human voice and man-made instrument—adoring the Christ Child, resurrecting all their bittersweet yesterdays, finding hope for all their tomorrows.

The harmonica slid freely over Alton's lips, its path moistened by his hot, salty tears. Then, when he thought he could bear it no longer, blessedly the song ended.

Miss Abby continued to stare out the window—contemplating the stars as if seeking the one that had guided the Wise Men.

Shaken, Alton stumbled from the cabin, tore, coatless, through the snow and wind, and flung himself into the very barn where he'd raised that foot-stomping, hand-clapping music with Will.

But that time had passed.

And a new one awaited him.

Throwing himself down before the manger, he laid his arms on the rough boards, sank his head onto them, and sobbed.

It seemed an eternity before he lifted his face. Then he saw Jem, quietly watching him.

"Come, Pa," Jem said. "It's time to go in."

Alton shook his head. "No, son. Miss Buckner will think I'm a fool."

Jem's eyes filled with tears. "No, Pa. She'll understand. I think she understands—everything. She's suffered, too, you know."

"I'll be along in a moment," Alton agreed, sighing.

"We'll be waiting," Jem said softly and disappeared into the night.

Alton looked up into a blackness broken only by the twinkling stars that had gleamed through the ages. *Perhaps those very stars had signaled the arrival of the Christ Child to a waiting world,* Alton thought. He stared at them, as if pleading for the heavens to part and reveal to him the answers he sought.

Was Miss Abby the woman the Lord had sent to him? His to recognize and claim? The one destined to become his cherished helpmate? Was she? Or was he attracted to her because she reminded him of his departed wife? Were the feelings true—or, like the stars, only a reflection of love for the woman he could never forget, never replace?

"Thy will be done," Alton murmured fervently and rose from his knees.

Then he strode to the cabin to face Jeremiah, Lizzie, the children . . . Abby.

chapter
12

ON A CLEAR Christmas Day, Alton transported the three little girls carrying the china dolls he'd purchased for their Christmas gifts, to the Preston farm.

After Lizzie's announcement the night before, he was not surprised to find Miss Buckner present, but in the wake of his tumultuous departure, he was pleasantly surprised to find that she treated him no differently from before.

Fanny's table was laden with evidence that she had been cooking for days in preparation of this feast, and the guests partook of the succulent meal in shifts.

Miss Buckner and Lizzie joined Fanny in the kitchen while the menfolk gathered around the hearth, talking, then later, playing games with the children. The afternoon passed pleasantly, with no mention of the embarrassing incident. And Alton breathed easily again.

"I 'spect we'd better be headin' home, little ones," Alton summoned the girls.

Reluctantly they put aside their toys and collected their wraps. Miss Buckner helped the youngsters into their coats and secured scarves snugly around small heads. Then, impulsively, she kissed each rosy cheek.

When she released them, Miss Abby rose abruptly. "I really

should be going, too," she said, blinking back tears. "That is, if Jem will be kind enough to take me back to my cabin."

"Perhaps Alton could drop Miss Abby off on his way home," Lizzie suggested smoothly.

"Why, o' course," Alton agreed. "It won't take but a minute or two to take the route by the schoolhouse. Fetch your wraps, Miss Abby. The girls an' I will be honored to see you safely home."

Miss Buckner gave him a twinkling smile. "My pleasure, I'm sure, Mister Wheeler." And, turning to her hosts, she said, "Many thanks for the most wonderful Christmas of my life. Until I moved to Salt Creek, I never knew how it felt to be part of a real family. You're all more precious to me than words can say."

"The feelin's are returned, Miss Abby, rest assured o' that!" Fanny said emphatically. "You're loved by ever'one in these parts."

Miss Abby frowned. "Well, perhaps not by everyone," she said carefully, and her eyes darkened as a shadow passed across them. "But by most folks, I should hope," she concluded in a bright tone.

Amid a flurry of farewells, Alton lowered the children into a hollow scooped out in the pile of straw, then lifted Miss Abby up to the seat beside him.

Homeward bound, the horses bobbed their heads, nickering as they clip-clopped over the frozen road and the wagon wheels thunked and clunked.

The sun slanted low in the sky, silhouetting the hardwood forests against the sky and casting a rosy glow across the snow-covered meadows. The air was bitterly cold but so still that the smoke from the chimneys rose in a thin, straight plume.

Alton had felt a trace of fear at the suggestion that he carry the schoolmarm home, but once on their way, he found conversation easy and pleasant.

"If you can spare a moment, Alton . . . I . . . I mean, Mister Wheeler," Miss Abby stammered, her cheeks flushing crimson, "I have a little treat for the girls."

"I 'spose we can tarry a spell," he decided, eying the approaching dusk. "But I'd like to get home before dark."

Hurriedly Miss Abby led them into the cabin. "This will take only a moment. Close your eyes, girls!" she ordered, building the suspense. From a small cupboard she withdrew an apothecary jar of candy sticks and balanced it in her hands. "Now you can open them!"

In unison, blue eyes widened when they beheld the gleaming jar filled with brightly colored candy sticks.

"You may each have two," Miss Abby said. "And if you suck them slowly, they'll last a long time!"

Molly, Marissa, and Katie selected their treats, and before Alton had to prompt them, they chorused, "Thank you, Miss Abby."

"They're all so dear, Mister Wheeler. You can be justly proud of them and of the job you've done. Bringing up the children alone hasn't been easy, I know."

Alton acknowledged the compliment with a humble nod. "I haven't been alone, 'though sometimes I've felt like it. Jem's lent a hand, an' Lizzie. Will an' Fanny, too. Most of all, I guess, I've had the good Lord to lean on."

"You girls have your papa bring you to see me again, all right?" Miss Abby invited. "And I'll promise to save some candy sticks for you."

Alton herded his charges to the wagon, tucking them in before he leaped to the spring seat and drove on. But he could feel her eyes on him, and finally he gave in to the overpowering urge to look over his shoulder.

When he did so, he saw the lonely, solitary form of Miss Abby, her fingers moving in a forlorn little wave that matched the wretched gesture of his three small girls as they bade her good-bye. They continued waving until he had rounded a bend in the road, and she was lost to view.

In the days following Alton came to terms with his loneliness, with the memories of Sue Ellen he had laid to rest in Jem's barn on Christmas Eve. It appeared that he must be content with his lot—bringing up his little girls to know and love the Lord, taking pleasure in seeing them grow and learn day by day.

For although Alton was attracted to Miss Buckner, he was still unsure of the basis for that attraction. For her part, he suffered no illusions that she returned his feelings. Why, he was almost old enough to be her pa!

Always, Miss Abby treated him with polite respect, and when she chatted with him, treated Alton no differently from the other men in her presence. She bore herself with quiet dignity, befitting a schoolmarm's position.

Toward the middle of February, however, Alton felt a strain in their relationship. Miss Abby seemed less bubbly; her smiles, forced; her mind, preoccupied; the set of her lips, grimly fixed.

Concerned, Alton finally dared broach the subject with Lizzie one day when she was rolling out sugar cookies, patiently suffering the help of tiny hands as they fashioned the creations into valentines and glazed them with frosting tinged pink with wild strawberry jam.

"Does it strike you folks that Miss Buckner's been a wee tad distant, Lizzie?" Alton asked quietly. "Or is it my imagination?"

Lizzie glanced up at him, twisting her wrist as she formed

172

another cookie. She chewed on her lip, obviously pondering a reply.

"It's not your imagination, Alton," Lizzie said, sighing. "In fact, Mama and I are plumb scared Miss Abby's goin' to quit."

"Quit?!" Alton yelped. "But why? She seems to like it here. She spoke as if she was satisfied with her wages. The students like her, and she seems to really cotton to them."

Lizzie slid a tin of cookies from the oven, then tapped her foot as she waited a few seconds for them to grow firm before removing them to the oilcloth.

"Not all of them," she said archly. "Oh, maybe they really do like Miss Abby. But if so, they've got some mighty peculiar ways of showin' it. Some of the older boys have been up to a lot of devilment. She feels perhaps a gentleman teacher might be more in order. Maybe Miss Abby is too kindhearted."

"More'n most," Alton acknowledged.

"With what Miss Abby's been through in her life, well, poor dear, she hates to hurt others, and, also, she's not as confident about people as she could be. Understandable, I reckon, her bein' a stranger and havin' to fend for herself. I expect maybe she just doesn't know how to take the boys' tomfoolery."

"Boys will be boys," Alton said. "When she confessed her troubles to you, no doubt she'd just had a bad day."

"Maybe so," Lizzie said, unconvinced that it was true.

An hour later Alton called a yawning Molly and Marissa from their play and suggested he take them home.

"Let them nap here, if you like, Alton," Lizzie said. "Jem an' Pa must've gotten delayed somewhere along the trail 'tween here an' Watson. I promised Maylon, Thad, and Lester I'd send valentine cookies to the school for a treat. Would you mind droppin' off the box of cookies at the schoolhouse? Otherwise the young'uns will be so disappointed—"

"I'll do it," he agreed readily. "'Twon't take long, and I'll leave the girls, if you're sure they'll not be a bother."

"No bother a'tall," Lizzie said, gently placing the cookies in a box lined with leftover Christmas tissue. "Lay these on the straw," she cautioned. "They break easily."

The drive to the schoolhouse afforded Alton rare moments to admire the subtle changes in the landscape wrought by the changing seasons, think his thoughts without interruption, and enjoy a few moments of aloneness without feeling so lonely.

But nearing the school building, Alton was jolted abruptly from his contemplation by the sound of raucous laughter, muffled shouts, and banging desks. *What in tarnation is going on in that classroom?* he wondered, jerking the team to a halt and covering the path to the door in a few swift strides.

There was no answer to his knock nor to his call, for the racket within. But when he twisted the knob, then kicked the door wide, filling the entrance with his powerful presence, silence thundered.

Several pairs of eyes, wide with fear, turned in his direction.

"You young pups have been raised in God-fearin', Christian homes," he bellowed, "and know the difference 'tween right an' wrong. Now! Turn to your books and let this be the end of your devilment, or I'll arrange for you to be answerin' to your pa and ma for your conduct! Now, I say!"

At his command, heads bowed to confront slates and texts.

Finally Alton spoke again. "Miss Abby, I'll be needin' your help, if you can spare a minute of your time."

Taking a deep breath, Miss Abby drew herself to her full height, patting a few flyaway strands of honeyed hair. She gave a weak smile, then clutched up her cloak, which she spun around her, and hugged it tightly into place.

Alton led Miss Abby outside. He'd meant to take her to the

174

wagon, give her the cookies, then explain that she should judge whether or not to distribute them as a valentine treat or withhold them a day or two to serve as a reward for better behavior.

But once outside the classroom, Miss Abby's brave composure crumpled. Alton heard the soft sniffle and turned toward her, his heart dropping to his feet as she began to sob brokenly.

"Now, now, don't take on so, Miss Abby. They're only young upstarts," Alton soothed. "They don't mean nothin' by their foolery."

Gently Alton led the quaking young woman to the sparse woods on the bluff overlooking Salt Creek and seated her on a large boulder. While only a few steps from the schoolhouse, the spot was out of earshot of the students. Here Miss Abby could cry out her frustration without fear of being overheard.

While he'd meant only to console her with a clumsy pat on the shoulder, Alton hadn't realized that tears had been crowding her eyes all day, and at his kind words and tender gesture, the floodgates opened. The next moment, to his great surprise, Abby was in his arms, pressed against his chest, her blond curls tickling the base of his throat. Unable to restrain himself, he dropped a comforting kiss on her sweetly scented hair, which went unnoticed by the distraught young woman.

"Now, now, it'll pass," Alton comforted her. "It's not so bad, Miss Abby. You're just keyed up. Those boys are sufferin' from cabin fever and badly hankerin' for spring. 'Twarn't nothin' to go to pieces over."

"No," Abby protested, "it *won't* pass! There's much more to it than that!"

As Alton listened, a flood of personal failings flowed from her lips. "Maybe I'm not meant to be a teacher," she wailed softly. "I was no doubt a fool to believe I could—just because

175

I can read and cipher! But the offer of a teaching job seemed like the answer to my prayers. Being turned away from the orphans' home when I became too old to stay on—where on earth was I to go? No one wanted me!" She glared up at Alton as if he were part of the world that had rejected her.

"There are but a few ways a woman alone can make a living," she dropped her eyes self-consciously, "and most of them not respectable nor fitting for a Christian woman." Then she lifted her head with a defiant toss and her eyes blazed. "I intend to resign my position here at once—today! But, don't worry, I'll find some way to earn my keep!"

Alton was galvanized into action at the idea of this petite woman being rudely snatched away from them, uprooted and transplanted elsewhere—who knew where? It would be a crying shame to lose her, Alton thought, when she had come to mean so much to so many people in the community—to his children—to *him!* The notion struck him with the force of a mule's kick to the midsection.

"No!" Alton cried out. "You can't do that, Abby—uh, *Miss* Abby! We need you!" he yelped. "There's been nary a complaint about your performance as our young'uns' teacher. You can't leave—you're so important to my little Katie. Why, she'd grieve so if you left . . . her, without a mama of her own. Please promise me that you'll at least stick it out to the end of the school term!"

Abby stared out over the valley. The last vestiges of winter still clung tenaciously to the land, but here and there, where the snow had melted, was a faint glimpse of green. Spring would come—eventually.

"I . . . I would like to, but—" She shrugged helplessly and gestured toward the school building that had swelled with laughter and hoots.

"Don't you worry your head about those rowdy young

rapscallions," Alton ordered. "After the tongue-lashin' they just got from me, I daresay you'll not be havin' any more trouble. And, if you do, they know I won't shrink from takin' it up with their pas. You have to remember that boys' blood runs high in the spring of the year—" Then he blushed to hear himself speaking like that to a young woman—unwed, at that.

"I suppose that's so," she murmured weakly.

"They meant no offense. They're like spirited young colts, kickin' up their heels. Why, I'll wager they'd hide their heads in shame to think their shenanigans had you ready to resign."

"I suppose so, but—"

"But it hurts," Alton finished for her.

She regarded him with reddened eyes. "Yes!" She cried out in a anguished whisper. "Yes, it hurts. Terribly. How did you—"

Her words faded away. Alton took her soft hand in his and squeezed it encouragingly.

"I know what hurtin' is all about, Abby," he explained gently. "When we hurt the very worst, when unhappiness is like a dull ache that won't go away, that's when it's the very hardest to keep on tryin', or find the will to even want to. An' that's when the Lord expects us to turn to Him. Give Him your problems, Abby. Let Him handle 'em for you."

"I'll try," Abby promised weakly. "I guess that in my hurt and unhappiness, I've forgotten to trust in Him."

"I'll be prayin' for you," Alton said. "And askin' Lizzie, Jem, Fanny, and Will to put in a word for you, too."

"Thank you, Mister Wheeler—" Abby said.

Alton extended his hand to help her from the boulder. As he did, her toe hooked on a root and she fell forward heavily. Instinctively Alton grasped her arm, his other hand sliding around her slim waist.

When his hand accidentally cleaved between cloak and prim blouse, Alton felt the warmth of her beneath his fingertips, and he recoiled, startled, from the reaction it provoked in him. Then, before he could stop himself, he was holding her close.

He hadn't meant for it to happen—and he was sure Miss Abby hadn't either—but as she looked up at him, about to utter appreciation, he captured her tender lips in a warm and gentle kiss.

Suddenly the movement of the world seemed to cease, other humanity disappeared to a netherworld, leaving them alone, trusting and clinging to one another, sharing their hurts and discovering forgotten joys.

"Abby . . . I'm sorry . . . I'm so sorry!" Alton murmured.

Then he broke away guiltily, silently chastising himself for taking advantage of a woman's weakness and giving in to his own manly desires.

She backed away rapidly, putting distance between them. "Oh, no! It wasn't at all your fault. I stumbled . . . and, well . . . I don't know what came over me to behave like that."

Abruptly Alton changed the subject, mentioning the freshly baked cookies. "I don't know if you want to give 'em to the pupils today, or save 'em a spell until you feel they're more deservin' of a treat."

Miss Abby accepted the box of cookies. "I'll let them enjoy Lizzie's cookies while they're fresh. Perhaps we can use them to celebrate a sort of . . . covenant . . . a new commitment for me to teach to the best of my ability, and the students to learn just as earnestly."

"That's a fittin' idea," Alton said.

She looked up at him. "If you don't mind, Mister Wheeler," she said softly. "If you could step in and witness the covenant, perhaps there'd be no cause for you to have to take the young

178

men to task before their fathers. A bit of faith and trust might accomplish more than harsh words and punishment."

"I'd be honored," Alton agreed. "To be truthful, I had little relish to take bad news to the young'uns' folks. But for your sake, Miss Abby, I'd have done it."

"Let's try this, instead."

Alton watched, and his heart swelled with awesome pride as Abby, so slight, slim, and pretty in her fair way, stepped to the front of the class, and in a voice that didn't tremble the least, explained the terms of her proposition.

"Your agreement will spare your friend and neighbor, Mister Wheeler, from journeying to your individual homes to confront your parents with an account of your rude behavior." She lowered her voice. "I don't want that, nor, I'm sure, do you." The classroom was still as a tomb. "Are we agreed?" she asked quietly.

A soft murmur of affirmation rippled through the room.

"Then we will mark our covenant with a celebration—a Valentine party! Maylon, Lester, and Thad, would you pass out the cookies your mama has baked and decorated for us?"

Alton turned to leave but Abby's voice halted him. "Stay for the party, Mister Wheeler, if you would. School will be over shortly and you can drive Lizzie's children and Katie home."

Alton nodded, then folded his large frame onto a vacant bench. He felt a strange sting of disappointment. For an instant he'd dared hope that Abby had requested him to stay because she wanted him present—wanted him with her in the same unexplainable way he wanted to remain with her. But, of course, it was only his wishful thoughts that caused him to harbor that paltry hope. For all her youth, she was a wise and practical woman, who was thinking of the children's welfare—not of him.

He watched her—while trying not to be obvious about it—and his heartbeat slowed with an unpleasant sense of lonely despair. She hadn't glanced in his direction—not once! After the way he'd stolen a kiss from her, she probably couldn't bear to look at him. Had him labeled a rake. A cad. And a doddering old fool, to boot!

Alton munched one of Lizzie's cookies and swallowed it without being conscious of the taste. He was thankful when it was time to go and was only aware the moment had finally arrived when Maylon, Lester, Thad, and Katie were at his side, eager to leave.

"Thank you for dropping by, Mister Wheeler!" Abby sang out. "And come back! You're welcome any time—"

So steeped in humiliation and heartache was he that Alton was deaf to her plea. Flushing as the eyes of the older students turned to regard her, Miss Abby brusquely began cleaning the chalkboard.

By the time Alton had settled the children in the wagon and taken his seat, he had almost willed himself to believe the afternoon—the kiss—had never taken place. He dared not even honor his word to her that he'd ask prayer for her dilemma.

Besides, Alton sighed, both situations were under control—the one in the classroom and the one outside, the need to love and be loved.

chapter
13

"Pa . . ."

Katie's soft voice—a whimper—startled Alton.

He pivoted to face her, his dark brows shooting up in question. Puzzled, he held the paring knife poised over the potato he was peeling to add to the mound in the kettle to be boiled for their supper along with the pork that hissed in the cast-iron skillet.

From behind her back Katie produced a folded note, affixed with sealing wax. She held it out to him as if it were loathsome to touch.

Alton set the knife aside, the potato beside it, and wiped his hands on a fraying towel.

He cast Katie an assessing glance, wondering, with a knifing flash of concern, what this was all about. Instead of arriving home with a bound, banging the door behind her and bouncing in to give him a hug, she'd stolen in, quiet as a mouse.

Indeed, he hadn't even heard the door open. Katie had carefully eased herself in so that the hinges wouldn't whine to announce her presence, then crept across the floor, avoiding the planks that creaked.

Now she was looking up at Alton, note extended in

trembling hand, her eyes luminous with unshed tears. Blinking quickly, Katie turned away when Alton accepted the crisply folded piece of stationery.

For a hopeless moment Alton thought it might be a social summons for him to appear at the schoolhouse, giving him an excuse to see Miss Abby. Immediately he banished the thought.

Hadn't she been distant to him at church lately? Distant even to her beloved Katie, who no longer clung and chattered to the schoolmarm as she once had but instead skulked safely out of reach?

Alton felt awash in embarrassment. Had he somehow so offended Miss Abby that she had rejected not only him but his child, as well?

Before he could loosen the sealing sax and unfold the note, Katie began to sob.

"I'm sorry, Pa," she bawled. Her face crumpled into tears. Clutching her slate to her, she lurched for the door.

"Katie! Stop! What's going on? What in tarnation did you do to cause Miss Abby to send a note home?"

Alton felt a helpless flow of sympathy when he saw the stricken look on Katie's mute face. Sighing, he unfolded the paper and smoothed it flat, bracing himself for the truth.

"Dear Mister Wheeler . . . ," began the note, written in Miss Abby's fine, feathery script, "I regret that it has become necessary for me to bring an unpleasant matter to your attention. I fear that Katie has become a problem in the classroom, although I have taken private counsel with her. Now, I have no choice but to appeal to you as her father—"

Alton's eyes staggered and tripped over the words, lurching back and forth between the lines.

He was consumed by hot anger and burning shame.

He felt like a fool!

Alton's mind reeled with the memory of the heated lecture he'd delivered the erring boys on Valentine's Day. Echoing mockingly through his thoughts, were his exact words as he promised Miss Abby that there'd be no further problems!

And now he held in his hands evidence that further troubles plagued the poor woman. And the galling fact was that the troublemaker was his own daughter!

With a muttered oath, Alton balled the crisp paper in his hand, then cast it from him, flinging it across the room. His troubled face registered the gamut of conflicting emotions waging war within him. Shame. Anger. Annoyance. Pity. Confusion . . . But he could not act. Instead, he sat motionless, stupified, while Katie nervously shifted her weight from one scuffed shoe to the other.

Alternately he considered bending Katie over his knee and warming her backside good and proper, but before he could, he was overcome by the piteous desire to pull her into his embrace, hold his bearded cheek against her hair, and cry with her.

Oh Lord! Alton pleaded for guidance.

Eventually all remnants of fury evaporated. When he was in control of his senses enough to face Katie, he saw a small, frightened child, her eyes duplicating Sue Ellen's endless love that lingered, sustaining him, even in his loneliness and frustration.

Obeying a small voice within, he drew the child to him, cradling her in his arms but willing himself to speak firmly.

"Are you aware o' the meanin' of this note, Mary Katharine Wheeler?"

Katie ducked her chin and lowered her eyes. Her nod was barely perceptible. A pigtail bobbed slightly.

"Yes, sir," she breathed. "Miss Abby told me she was taking up the matter of my behavior with you, Pa."

"Didn't you hear the lecture I delivered to the young pups causin' Miss Abby grief? You took the covenant to obey and behave the same as the rest of them, didn't you, Katie? And now I receive word that you're no better'n those scamps. An' what's worse—you failed to keep your word to Miss Abby."

"I'm sorry, Pa."

"As good as Miss Abby's been to you, an' as much as I thought you'd taken a likin' to her, I'm surprised you could find it in yourself to give her pain when she was doin' her level best to help you learn and be somebody someday—like your mama."

"I'm sorry, Pa," Katie repeated when he paused for breath.

"You've got some fine explainin' to do! Why have you been causin' Miss Abby torment?"

Alton's question seemed to vibrate in the air. Katie squirmed away from him.

"I . . . ummm . . . just *'cause.* . . ."

Alton shook her. "You'd better come up with a better answer than that!" he thundered in exasperation. "This ain't like you, Kate. Not like you a'tall. Now I want the truth! Why'd you do the ornery things you've done?"

A hiccoughing sob exploded from Katie. She bolted for Alton, clinging to him, begging understanding as her eyes puddled with tears.

"I did it for you!" Katie wailed her confession. "I know I promised Miss Abby, along with the rest of the students, not to cause further devilment. An' I didn't like what I had to do 'cause I could tell it hurt her bad, Pa. It made me feel plumb awful to have her angry with me. But I did it, Pa, so you'd have an excuse to go see Miss Abby in private. You'd *have* to go if she sent a note home."

It had been the reply least anticipated by Alton. The childish rationale left him without immediate reply. When he recognized the twisted logic, he struggled, suspended between the urge to laugh or bellow with rage.

Incredulous anger born of humiliation won out.

"Thunderation!" Alton exploded. "That's the sneakiest, most underhanded notion I ever heard—*why?*" His raging changed direction. "Why, Katie? I want to know why it's so important to you to have me meet with Miss Abby that you have to get into trouble to guarantee that it happens. Don't we see her every week at church?" A whimper from the bedroom signaled that he'd awakened one of the napping twins. He lowered his voice. "*Why?*" he asked again, his breath whistling between his teeth.

Katie avoided his burning glare, shrinking from him. "I reckoned that if maybe you saw Miss Abby more . . . then you'd start lovin' Miss Abby like I love her." Katie rubbed her fists into her eyes, smearing teary grime across her red cheeks. She gave a soft snuffle. "I hoped, then, that maybe you'd start lovin' Miss Abby, Pa, like Miss Abby loves you."

Alton gaped. What did she—a child—know about love? That kind of love between a man and a woman? And how, in the name of Pete, could she begin to know that Abby loved him when he'd been so careful to shield from the world, from Abby, and even from himself, that he cared for the schoolmarm more than for any woman since Sue Ellen.

Questions crowded Alton's mind—questions that demanded—yearned for—immediate answers.

Alton struggled to keep his voice calm. "You say Miss Abby loves me, Kate. Are you sure?"

Katie nodded. "Yes, sir."

Alton drew her close. She lifted her innocent, trusting face to his. He tenderly smoothed a pigtail over her shoulder, capturing a stray wisp behind her ear.

"How can you know that, bein' just a child? Have you heard talk?"

Katie nodded. "Yes, sir."

"What's been said? I want to know!" Alton commanded in a desperate whisper.

Katie gave Alton an uncertain, almost cowering glance in the face of this desperation she could not understand. When she realized that the intensity of his emotions was not directed at her, she licked her lips, wrinkled her brow, and struggled to recollect what she'd heard.

"The older girls at school . . . they talk an' giggle 'bout things they've heard their ma and pa say. Lizzie an' Jem have said things, too, Pa. So have Lizzie and Fanny. I don't think they meant for me to hear. They never talked about it when you were near but would wait 'til you'd step out to the pump for a drink of water, or would leave to tend Doc and Dan. Then they'd shush up as soon as you got back."

Alton entertained a queer mixture of invasion and anticipation. He cleared his throat. "And just what have these folks been sayin' about me? About us . . . Miss Abby an' me?"

Alton pulled Katie to his lap. She straightened importantly and picked at the hem of her dress before primly smoothing it.

"Lizzie's been sayin' you're too blind to see what's common knowledge to all the neighbors. Jem laughs that you're lucky you won't be found courtin' too slow, but only 'cause Miss Abby doesn't hold interest in any other man 'though she's careful to keep her feelings hid. Or at least tries to."

"I see," Alton said.

"An' the schoolchildren . . . they talk 'bout how Miss Abby comes to their houses for a meal . . . an' blushes like fury when someone chances to mention your name."

"Is that a fact?" Alton mused.

186

"Back along about Christmas time, I heard Lizzie and Fanny talkin'—wonderin'—if they should step in and do something. Make kindlin', or somethin', they called it. Had to do with buildin' a fire."

Alton frowned thoughtfully. "Wouldn't have been a wee bit o' *matchmakin'* now, would it?"

"*That's* the word!" Katie cried in recognition. "The other week they said they weren't going to do nothin' else 'til the school term ended. That's how long they 'lowed as they'd give you to take up with Miss Abby on your own after you came to school on Valentine's Day. After listenin' to them . . . I thought maybe—"

"That you'd get in trouble at school so I'd have to go see Miss Abby an' we could fall in love like everybody's been expectin' us to do?"

"Yes, Pa," Katie admitted. "Please don't be angry. I love Miss Abby so much! I've been hopin' and prayin' you'd come to love her, too. Like I do. Like the twins do. Like 'most everyone does."

"Do you realize how much you hurt Miss Abby, doin' what you did?"

Katie nodded beneath the burden of her guilt. She faced Alton squarely. "Yes, sir," she admitted softly. "But I hoped that if you fell in love with Miss Abby, then I could tell her an' she'd understand and be glad I did!"

"Katie . . . Katie," Alton sighed. "You should never do something bad in the vain hope that someday somethin' good will come of it."

"I'm sorry, Pa," Katie murmured a final time.

"Now get into some clean clothes. Then help me dress the babies." He set her firmly on her feet, then rose, stroking his beard thoughtfully.

"Where are we goin'?"

187

"We're drivin' to Miss Abby's cabin so you can apologize to her for your misdeeds and beg her pardon."

Katie froze. "What about chorin', Pa?" she reminded, consulting the clock pointedly.

"Chorin' can wait, Mary Katharine. Apologies can't."

"All right, Pa," she sighed.

Silently she crept to the attic and made almost no noise as she donned a clean frock, patted her hair into place, then returned to help dress the sleepy toddlers Alton had roused from their nap.

Between them they tugged and turned plump arms and legs, coaxing the babies, flushed with sleep, into warm, dry clothing.

Katie banked the fire in the hearth and herded Marissa and Molly outside. Alton quickly hitched the team. Only when he reached the fork in the road did his decision come clear, and he headed Doc and Dan in the opposite direction of the schoolhouse.

"I thought we were goin' by Miss Abby's," Katie said.

"Changed my mind," Alton said. "I'm droppin' you young'uns by Lizzie an' Jem's. Believe me, you'd better not cause them so much as a squeak of trouble. I dislike imposin', but I reckon I don't have much choice in the matter. I'm goin' to Miss Abby to apologize in private—tonight—and you can start plannin' what you'll say to beg her forgiveness first thing in the mornin' at school."

"Yes, Pa."

Lizzie, Jeremiah, and the children had just been seated for their evening meal when Alton and the three Wheeler children arrived.

"Katie got into a mite o' trouble with the schoolmarm. Miss Abby sent a note home with her. I figgered it best to meet with her right away so's we can nip this problem in the bud."

Jem asked a careful question or two, and Alton, his face scorching, admitted the truth. He wiped his brow with his hand. Just the brief gesture afforded Jem and Lizzie time to exchange a hurried, amused glance.

"Run along and set Miss Abby's heart at ease," Lizzie suggested. "Take what time you need. I'll feed your young'uns along with ours. An' I'll set a plate of food in the warmin' oven for your return."

Alton nodded his thanks. "Much obliged, Lizzie."

"Give Miss Abby our regards," she said.

Alton left the snug cabin with Jem in his wake. Alton climbed to the high spring seat, and Jem lingered near the hitch, his hand resting on the brake lever.

"Don't be too angry with Katie, Pa," Jeremiah begged on her behalf. "She was only doing what she thought best. Doubtless others would have taken matters into their own hands, to budge you two into action, if they'd figured how."

"It's true, then?" Alton asked. "That tongues have been waggin' about me—an' Miss Abby?"

Jeremiah nodded. "Yes, Pa. But not in the way of gossip. And not in a disparaging manner, comparing your age with Miss Abby's and finding it a joke. There had been natural curiosity and speculation by folks who love you both and want your happiness."

"I see," Alton said softly.

"It was bound to happen," Jeremiah went on. "Miss Abby's become a part of the community. We're all fond of her. It's right that folks hope she'll stay on and teach in our school. There's been some idle gossip that she was upset and had cause to want to leave. Then you set things right in her classroom. That sparked some loose talk—that maybe your feelings for her and hers for you—would give just reason for her to remain."

"She's not goin' to leave, is she?" Alton asked suddenly.

Jeremiah shrugged. "It's only talk," Jem said. "No one's dared ask for fear they'd hear bad news."

Alton gathered the reins and snapped them across the Clydesdales' rumps. "I'll be back after I attend to the business at hand, son."

"Our prayers are riding with you, Pa."

Alton turned the team onto the road, retracing his path. The horses, knowing the way, picked through the ruts and holes in the winding road that crawled up and down, through and around, the hills and hollows.

Steeped in reflective thought, Alton prickled with the realization that he had been too blind to see what was so clear to those around him—even to his young daughter.

At the thought of Miss Abby's leaving the area, his heart constricted and he felt consumed by a wretched hollowness that all but paralleled the void created when Sue Ellen was lost to him.

On her deathbed Sue Ellen had told him that love would be his again, that someday it would find a place in his heart. She'd made him promise that he would allow himself to experience the return of joy. Promise that he'd not flee love if it came his way again.

With reluctance he'd tendered his vow. Now he knew the time had come. As he had withdrawn into himself, ignoring the talk swirling about him, love had sought him out relentlessly, demanding his recognition—his answer.

Through the bounty of the Lord's grace, Alton found himself keeping his promise to Sue Ellen, but quite apart from his own efforts. Suddenly he felt newly alive with joy! He loved Miss Abby! He did!

He had come to admire her first as a valued member of the community—the teacher they had long been seeking for their young'uns. As she had begun to take an interest in his little Katie, loving the child as her own, Alton had found in her a trusted friend and true.

But it was not those qualities he was thinking of now. He remembered the sweet pliancy of her lips on his, after which even Lizzie's cookies tasted flat upon his tongue. He not only loved Miss Abby as a woman, he desired to make her his wife!

Then his inward rejoicing became a dull, agonizing ache, extinguishing the flame of belief that flared brightly in the hope that she could belong to him. What if they were wrong? What if the talk and innuendo had been one distortion feeding another? What if they were wrong about her supposed love for him? How would he ever bear it?

"Oh Lord . . . please," Alton begged. "I've come this far. Work in Miss Abby's heart the miracle you've worked in mine."

chapter

14

ALTON'S TREPIDATION increased with every clip-clop of the horses' hooves. Flicking their ears and bobbing their heads, they plodded on, conquering the narrow trail. Too soon, it seemed, they were drawing up to the deserted school building, with Miss Abby's small dwelling nearby, a comforting plume of smoke rising from the chimney.

Alton's pulse quickened. Blood pounded through his temples, and there was a coppery taste on his tongue.

When he'd left Jeremiah, he had felt confident that he would know what to say. Now, a few breaths away from a confrontation with Miss Abby, all thought and analysis seemed expunged from his memory, as his tongue became a thick and lifeless thing. Even when he swallowed hard and licked his lips, the action seemed insufficient to prime the wellspring of coherent speech.

Alton hopped from the wagon and peered around. The schoolgrounds were ominously quiet.

A light, early spring breeze rifled the branches overhead. Limbs had grown knobby with the first buds of new life. Beneath the brown grass, fresh sprouts of green strained to emerge.

Alton wrapped the worn reins into a knot around the brake

handle and advanced toward the front door of Miss Abby's cabin. His boot heels echoed dully. Spasms of nervousness invaded the base of his stomach, making him feel almost queasy at the prospect of the task at hand.

Relief flooded over him when he heard the faint *chunk-chunk* of a pole ax, biting into wood as Miss Abby chopped kindling behind the cabin.

He rounded the small dwelling, halting as he watched the slight woman attack the seasoned oak, splintering off wood chips. Frustration marred her pretty face.

"Here! Let me do that!" Alton offered kindly, staring at the ground as he approached, the better to avoid meeting her gaze.

Abby straightened, putting one hand to her back and, with the other, shielded her eyes from the slanting rays of the sun.

Wordlessly Alton took possession of the ax, unintentionally brushing against her forearm. The cool, lifeless handle was worn as smooth as Abby's skin that was silken, warm, and so vitally alive beneath his touch.

At this brief contact she recoiled, and Alton's heart seemed to land at his feet with a despairing thud. Nor was the look of dismay that settled over her pretty features lost on him. He hadn't expected that, although he might have anticipated her gasp of surprise and the faint cry of alarm she uttered when she became aware of his presence.

Alton hoisted the ax and fell to chopping with deft blows.

Abby knelt and gathered her full skirt to form a functional basket. When Alton set aside the ax, her cheeks were flushed although her fair complexion was drained of color. Whether from exertion or fright, her heart was pounding visibly beneath the high neck of her proper white blouse.

Seeming to sense the direction of his gaze, Abby arose quickly, dizzily. Feeling faint, she touched her fingertips to

194

her breast. "You gave me such a start, Mister Wheeler!" she explained weakly. "I didn't expect to see you so soon . . . about the note, that is."

"I was too troubled to put it off, Miss Abby. Katie has never been one to cause problems—," Alton admitted.

"Perhaps we can discuss the matter over tea," Abby invited.

"That would be right pleasant," Alton agreed.

Abby hesitated. "Unless," she suggested carefully, "it would be unwise for me to entertain a gentleman in my private quarters. A lady alone can't be too careful—can't afford talk—"

Her face drenched crimson.

Alton stared at a spot of ground between his boots. "I fear there wouldn't be no more talk than has been goin' on already, Miss Abby," he said ruefully, lifting his gaze to meet hers.

A low moan of grief escaped her and she seemed to wilt before his eyes. "Oh, dear . . . I was afraid of that." Her lower lip quivered and she regarded Alton with a look of anguish in her blue eyes.

"My Katie's been one o' them," Alton confessed. He followed her into the neat, sparsely furnished cabin. "For that, I'm powerful sorry. But I can't find it in my heart to fault her too much—and you may have to forgive me for that—for arrangin' this meetin' between us . . . Abby."

At the curious admission, Abby wheeled abruptly. Gripping the blackened tea kettle, she stared, then with a brisk movement set it above the flames.

"Arranged, Mister Wheeler? I'm afraid I don't understand. Did I hear you correctly—*arranged*?"

"That you did," Alton affirmed.

Dazed, she seated herself across from him at the table. Alton avoided her eyes, preferring to examine the dancing

195

flames that hissed at the damp tea kettle. In measured tones he relayed Katie's scheme, one which neither of them had fathomed.

"That's why my young'un's been a trial and trouble to you, Abby. She didn't mean any harm—I tell you true. She's done what she has out of a misguided sense of love for you . . . and because she loves and cares about her ol' Papa."

"How sad . . ." And the lovely sapphire eyes filled with tears.

"I think I can promise you that Katie won't give you another moment's concern. Please accept my apology—"

Abby sprang from her chair, presenting her back to Alton as she busied herself with the fire.

"Don't be sorry," she said, so softly that Alton found himself straining to catch her words. "*I'm* not."

Her blurted admission leaped between them with a life of its own, and Alton's heart galloped wildly in response.

"Abby—" he murmured.

She refused to face him. "I wasn't aware that my most private feelings were as transparent as glass, making visible to all what I treasured most. Alton, I—I mean, Mister Wheeler, if any apologies are required, then they shall be mine! I certainly didn't intend that my love for your children—and yes, for *you*—should become a source of embarrassment."

The teakettle was forgotten. It boiled and bubbled a melodic accompaniment to Abby's tortured confession. But once begun, there was no stopping until her secret was out.

Tears splashed to her cheeks. "You can't imagine how I've admired you—a man who would do all you've done for your little girls, without one word of complaint. My respect for you has known no bounds. Being an orphan, perhaps I appreciate more than most such sacrificial love."

"Miss Abby—" Alton felt as if he should respond, but with

196

the intensity of her declaration, he remained almost robbed of speech.

"Perhaps I'm to be faulted, but with a life as devoid of love as mine, can I be blamed for dwelling on the attributes of a fine, upstanding man who offers all that a Christian woman could ever seem to desire?" She shuddered and squeezed her eyes against a fresh tide of tears. "All of my life, I've had so much love to give, Mister Wheeler, but no one to give it to— and no one who wanted it. Katie, Molly, and Marissa are so sweet and docile, so affectionate and trusting. It has been easy to lavish upon them all the love in my heart—to coddle them almost as if they were my own. Sometimes, in the most precious moments of my heart, I dreamed that they *were* mine . . . that someday . . . oh, forgive me!"

Abby ended her litany, unwilling to humiliate herself further.

Alton took a step toward her. She retreated. Then, believing her to swoon, he reached out and whirled her into his arms.

Her fluffy hair, billowing in disarray from the effects of the breeze and her efforts with the ax, caressed his cheek. His lips approached the shell perfection of her dainty ear.

"Did you say . . . you love me?" Alton whispered.

He felt her stiffen in instinctive denial, then go weak in helpless acknowledgment of the truth.

"Yes!" Abby gasped shamelessly. She turned, attempting to free herself of Alton's embrace. "Yes, I love you even though I never deluded myself that my love was returned. I have prayed to be free of this torment." She dropped her head miserably. "You can see that I have no choice but to leave."

Abby wrenched herself away. This time he let her go, watched her cross the room stiffly as if unmindful of her surroundings. Alton removed the screaming kettle from the fire.

"Abby . . . Miss Abby . . . you're wrong. You were wrong all along," Alton said.

Like a scalded cat she turned on him. "Don't you think I know that?" she cried. "Of course I know it was wrong. But I'm only human—a woman. I can't help it that I want what other women have—a home, a good man, children. The pain I feel in my heart is brutal enough without your heaping further humiliation upon me." She paused. "Mister Wheeler . . . would you please go now?"

"Humiliation?!" Alton yelped.

The unexpected criticism seared his mind, and mentally he retreated to inventory his words. What in tarnation had he said to widen the chasm between them?

She had been wrong, yes. But wrong about his intents, not wrong in her desires. The unintentional hurt caused by his innocent words made her pain his own and provoked a fresh surge of protective love for the young woman who had felt unwanted all of her years.

Abby hadn't the strength to resist when Alton approached and placed his arms around her. He touched her chin with his fingertip. For a moment she rebelled, then allowed her face to be lifted to his. But her eyelids remained closed, tears escaping at the corners.

Alton carefully kissed away the salty moisture, then moved steadily along the wet trail that traveled down her cheek.

"Oh . . . don't . . . don't," Abby begged softly. She turned her face away, but it only better presented the other cheek to Alton's tender care. Then his lips were a breath away from capturing hers.

"You've misunderstood me, Miss Abby," Alton whispered. "I didn't mean that it was wrong of you to love me. Why the

Lord God Himself knows how undeservin' I feel! I only meant I was deeply honored that a good, decent, God-fearin' woman like yourself would hold me in such esteem."

"Alton . . . ," Miss Abby murmured. Her eyes opened wide to survey him in surprise—delighted, delicious, promise-fulfilling surprise. Her lips moved, but no sound issued from them.

"Let me finish." Alton pressed on quickly. "What you were wrong about was in thinkin' that the love you had for me wasn't returned. I do care for you, Abby. I love you! More than I thought I could—or ever would—love again. It took a child—my child—to show me the way. But know that you've had my love, too, Abby. I guess you always have—always will."

"Oh, Alton," Abby whispered. "You don't know how happy I am. How very happy."

"No happier than I, my darlin'!"

Further words were unnecessary. Alton's kiss set to rest forever any lingering doubts about his love for Abigail Buckner.

"Thank the Lord for you, Alton Wheeler!" Abby whispered tremulously. She leaned her head on his chest, her ear just above his wildly pounding heart. "Thanks be to Him for the happiness I've dreamed about, desired, and prayed would someday be mine—"

"*Ours,*" Alton corrected lovingly.

Laughing softly, almost recklessly, Alton delivered a solid hug that jerked the hairpins from Miss Abby's neat coronet and sent a golden wave of hair spilling about her shoulders.

For a moment she froze, then laughed with Alton at what the neighbors would think about the young schoolmarm and the eligible widower in such scandalizing disarray!

"I love you, Abby. How I love you, woman!"

"No more than I love you!" she promised.

Alton released Abby from his arms, then waited for her to get her cloak. There was a multitude of family and friends waiting, praying for their news.

She preceded him through the cabin door. He closed it behind them, knowing that one day soon—very soon—she would be coming to his cabin as his cherished bride, a beloved mother for his children.

He looked heavenward. The darkness of night had fallen, bringing with it an approving hush. The vastness of the skies gleamed with the light of the smiling moon and the twinkle of stars. All creation seemed to be rejoicing, as spring came to long-fallowed hearts.

Alton lifted Miss Abby to the seat. En route, he delivered an impulsive kiss to lips that curved in delight. The brief contact foretold a sweet pact of new love even as Alton remembered the old.

Once again he gazed at the heavens.

I've kept my word, Sue. He smiled. *I've kept my word.*